"I don't just want t... for you to forget."

A dark flush rode high on his cheekbones. He gazed into her eyes steadily for a few heartbeats, and then he pushed himself up and sat on the edge of the bed. "Get out of here, Shannon."

"Rafe…"

"Don't tell me you want to talk about it. Don't tell me you should never have come in here. And don't tell me we'll forget about all of this in the morning." He shot a frustrated look at her. "Because we won't. You have too much good sense for both of us, and I don't want to be reminded about that now. So go to bed."

She didn't look back as she left his room. She couldn't. Because if she did, she might forget she had any good sense at all.

Dear Reader,

"It was a high like no other," says Elaine Nichols. She's speaking, of course, about getting "the call." After numerous submissions, Elaine sold her first manuscript to Silhouette Special Edition and we're pleased to publish *Cowgirl Be Mine* this month—a reunion romance between a heroine whose body needs healing and a hero whose wounds are hidden inside. Elaine has many more Special Edition books planned, so keep an eye out for this fresh new voice.

And be sure to pick up all the novels Special Edition has to offer. Marrying the Bravo fortune heir granted the heroine custody of her son, but once the two are under the same roof, they're *unable* to sleep in separate beds, in Christine Rimmer's *The Marriage Conspiracy*. Then a hungry reporter wishes his tempting waitress would offer him a tasty dish of *her* each morning, in *Dateline Matrimony* by reader favorite Gina Wilkins.

What's *The Truth About Tate?* Marilyn Pappano tells you when her journalist heroine threatens to expose the illegitimate brother of the hero, a man who would do anything to protect his family. She hadn't giggled since her mother died, so *His Little Girl's Laughter* by Karen Rose Smith is music to Rafe Pierson's ears. And in Tori Carrington's *The Woman for Dusty Conrad,* a firefighter hero has returned to divorce his wife, but discovers a still-burning flame.

We hope you enjoy this month's exciting selections, and if you have a dream of being published, like Elaine Nichols, please send a self-addressed stamped query letter to my attention at: Silhouette Books, 300 East 42nd St, 6th floor, New York, NY 10017.

Best,

Karen Taylor Richman
Senior Editor

Please address questions and book requests to:
Silhouette Reader Service
U.S.: 3010 Walden Ave., P.O. Box 1325, Buffalo, NY 14269
Canadian: P.O. Box 609, Fort Erie, Ont. L2A 5X3

His Little Girl's Laughter

KAREN ROSE SMITH

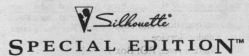

SPECIAL EDITION™

Published by Silhouette Books

America's Publisher of Contemporary Romance

ACKNOWLEDGMENTS

So many people helped me with research on this book. To Rose Foreman, who gave me insight into Equine Assisted Therapy; to Marlene Urso—my special California friend who has diverse information sources; to Mark Bradley, whose knowledge and experience helped me with accurate details; to firefighter Dominick Kass, whose expertise was invaluable. Thank you.

 SILHOUETTE BOOKS

ISBN 0-373-24426-6

HIS LITTLE GIRL'S LAUGHTER

Copyright © 2001 by Karen Rose Smith

This edition published by arrangement with Harlequin Books S.A.

® and TM are trademarks of Harlequin Books S.A., used under license. Trademarks indicated with ® are registered in the United States Patent and Trademark Office, the Canadian Trade Marks Office and in other countries.

Visit Silhouette at www.eHarlequin.com

Printed in U.S.A.

KAREN ROSE SMITH

has always been fascinated by horses. As a child, she visited her uncle's farm often and loved just watching the beautiful animals. She didn't actually learn to ride until she was a young adult. Then she became entranced by horses all over again, learning how intuitive they can be. An article in her local newspaper about Equine Assisted Therapy sparked the idea for this book.

Readers can write to Karen Rose at: P.O. Box 1545, Hanover, PA 17331.

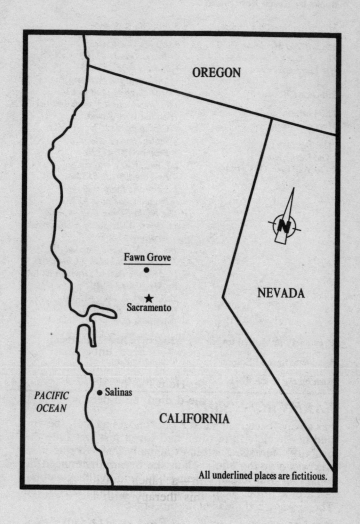

OREGON

NEVADA

Fawn Grove
●

★
Sacramento

PACIFIC
OCEAN

● Salinas

CALIFORNIA

All underlined places are fictitious.

Chapter One

On the lookout for a lane veering off the secondary road, Rafe Pierson slowed, turned his Lexus onto the gravel and glanced over at Janine.

For years, as a prosecuting attorney, his drive for success as well as justice had been unbeatable and unmatchable. But in the past eighteen months he'd lost his focus...and his edge. He'd lost his wife.

Ever since the day she'd died, he'd been losing his daughter, too.

He motioned ahead to the wooden arch with Rocky R engraved deeply into the wood. "We're here," he said, forcing a smile. This literally *was* the end of the road for both of them—a ranch outside of Fawn Grove, California. If this therapy with Dr. Shannon Collins didn't work...

His seven-year-old hardly lifted her chin, and he couldn't tell if she'd checked out the sign or not. She hadn't spoken a word since her mother had been gunned down by a man who'd wanted revenge on Rafe. Janine had witnessed it all.

Earlier Rafe had lowered the car windows to let the warmth, sights and sounds of June in northern California fill the silence between him and his daughter. Now a breeze blew strands of her shoulder-length hair along her cheek. It was as black as his, only finer and silkier. She had his green eyes, too, but these days when he tried to read what she was thinking, she avoided his gaze, as if she couldn't bear to let him see what was hidden there.

As he drove down the gravel lane, an old white-washed barn came into view. Across from it stood a two-and-a-half-story house, sided in light blue, with a rambling white wooden porch complete with an old-fashioned swing. This was a far cry from his contemporary ranch house back in Salinas.

After briefly scanning the other outbuildings, including a run-in shed for the three horses he counted in the pasture, he parked beside a tan pickup truck on a gravel area at the far side of the house. Beside a low-slung longer building stood a compact car. There was no activity anywhere. Rafe found that odd and checked his watch. It was 3:00 p.m.

Shannon Collins had told him she'd probably be in the corral when he arrived, but there was no one in the large corral beside the barn—no sign of life anywhere. Dr. Collins had promised him Janine would have a slow introduction to the Rocky R and to the equine assisted therapy that was her specialty.

With the practiced calm he'd struggled to perfect over the past eighteen months, he said to Janine, "Let's see if anyone's home."

He climbed out and came around to his daughter's door. After he opened it, she got out slowly and walked beside him up the path to the porch steps. When he rang the bell, he heard it chime inside, but no one answered the closed door. Opening the wooden screen, he rapped on the door—hard. That didn't bring anyone, either.

He'd never been a patient man. At least not when it came to getting what he wanted. Taking Janine's hand, he nodded toward the other buildings. "Let's take a look around and find somebody."

And if you can't find anyone? a voice in his head asked.

That was the million-dollar question. Janine had seen every specialist in the book—medical doctors, a psychiatrist who'd wanted to employ anti-depressants, a therapist she couldn't relate to. Finally he'd found another therapist who'd tried her best and who'd worked with Janine patiently, hoping for a breakthrough. But after nine months she'd felt she wasn't making any substantial progress and recommended a more unorthodox therapy—Shannon Collins's work.

Rafe remembered to slow his determined pace so Janine wouldn't have to run to keep up as they covered the distance to the long, low building. Knocking at that door also produced no results. As he grew more frustrated, he tamped down the anger that had been so much a part of him lately, unwilling to let Janine see it. They'd driven four hours from Salinas. He was sure she was thirsty and hungry, but she wouldn't tell him that. She wouldn't tell him anything.

"We might find horses in the barn," he suggested with false cheerfulness as he led her in that direction now. "Dr. Collins said her aunt has a dog, and kittens are always playing around the barn, too."

For a moment he thought he saw a spark of something in his daughter's eyes, but it was fleeting and gone before he could reassure himself it had been there.

Rafe pulled open the door on the side of the barn and stepped inside, Janine close behind him. He heard the soft murmur of a woman's voice and felt relieved. Guiding Janine through an open area stacked with hay bales and machinery, then down the walkway between the horse stalls, he suddenly stopped, realizing he should take his daughter right back outside. There was a chestnut mare lying in one of the stalls, covered with sweat, whinnying, while a beautiful young woman knelt by her head.

"Soon you'll have your baby, Dancer. Very soon." Rafe heard compassion in the young woman's voice.

As startled as he was by what was happening in front of his eyes, he registered everything about her— her curly, caramel-colored hair tied in a ponytail, her pretty face, her flowered knit shirt and blue jeans. He felt a visceral tug that took him completely by surprise.

"Oh, my. It's going to happen anytime now," came a soft whisper from a stall across the walkway. When Rafe turned toward the voice, he saw a woman with short blond and gray hair, who might be in her sixties, standing on a bale of hay inside the stall beside a teenager. The rough-looking boy had shaggy brown hair, an earring in his ear and a heavy metal band's logo on his T-shirt.

Although her attention seemed to be trained on the mare, the young woman must have been aware of

Rafe's presence. She raised her gaze to his. "Mr. Pierson?"

Her soft, dark-brown eyes as well as her gentle voice made his gut clench. The whole scene here did. Concerned Janine would be afraid, he put his hand on his daughter's shoulder.

"Dr. Collins?" he asked.

When she nodded, he nudged Janine around to go back outside. "I can see you're tied up. We'll wait at the house."

Where the therapist's voice had been questioning before, now it was firm. "You must be Janine." She looked directly at his daughter. Then she patted the mare's nose, quietly got to her feet, approached Janine and crouched down before her. "We can't talk loud or make lots of commotion, or Dancer might have trouble having her baby." She gestured to the woman and teenager. "That's why Aunt Cora and Clancy are over there," she added in a low voice.

"I don't think it's a good idea for Janine to see this," Rafe told her impatiently.

But Shannon Collins was studying his daughter. "Janine, my horse is going to have a baby. You can leave if you'd like...or you can stay and watch. If you want to stay and watch, I'll explain everything that's going to happen, so none of it will scare you."

"Dr. Collins..." Rafe warned.

Shannon stood and stepped very close to him...so close he could smell flowers...so close that his heart pounded...so close that her natural beauty jolted him like the shock of a Taser.

Her voice was almost a whisper, but he could hear her clearly. "Your daughter's therapy starts here and now. She'll be fine if she *wants* to stay and if she understands exactly what's happening.''

Rafe realized Shannon Collins's soft voice and feminine appearance had given him the wrong first impression. It was unlike him to have miscalculated. He kept his tone as low as hers and just as determined. ''I don't think she needs to see any more trauma.''

''The birth of a foal isn't trauma, Mr. Pierson. It's one of life's miracles.'' She glanced at Janine, who'd taken a few steps closer to Dancer. ''I think your daughter might know that.''

He was wrong to have brought Janine here. When he had first heard about equine assisted therapy, psychotherapy utilizing a patient's interaction with horses, he'd considered it pure quackery. But Dr. Shannon Collins had come highly recommended. He'd studied and checked her credentials. Yet if she was going to contradict him, if she thought *she* was the one to decide what was best for his daughter—

Dancer grunted and moved restlessly.

Janine took a step back but still kept watch.

''Ask her,'' Shannon advised him. ''Ask her if she wants to stay.''

This wasn't at all what Rafe had envisioned in coming here, not a war of wills from the first moment he smelled hay. But then Janine raised her gaze to his and really looked at him for the first time in weeks. The words came unbidden to his lips. ''Do you want to stay?''

She nodded slowly.

There was no hint of triumph on Shannon's face as she crouched down before Janine again. ''My name's Shannon, and we're going to be spending some time together in the days to come. But for right now, you and your dad will have to watch from over there with Aunt Cora and Clancy. All right?''

Janine nodded again, and Shannon smiled at her. It was a smile, Rafe thought, that assured anyone who saw it that the world was a good place.

He knew better. So did his daughter.

Still, Janine seemed to accept the hope. He held his hand out to her to let her know he was here to protect her...that even though they were in a strange place, she could still count on him. When she took his hand, he led her to the stall, and she climbed onto a bale of hay so she could see what was happening.

The teenager took one look at Rafe, then moved to the other side of the older woman, shifting another bale over so he could stand on it.

The elderly lady, who looked as if a good wind could blow her into the next county, smiled at him. ''I'm Cora,'' she said, keeping her voice low. ''Shannon's aunt.'' She nudged the boy next to her with her shoulder. ''And this is Clancy. He helps out on the Rocky R.''

Rafe had an immediate and sure conviction that there was more to Clancy's story than that, but he nodded to Cora and introduced himself and his daughter.

''I know who you are,'' Cora said. ''Shannon told me she was expecting you.''

Suddenly Janine started and looked down. Rafe wondered why until he saw the golden retriever who'd come from the rear of the stall to smell Janine's leg. She'd been startled, but now she studied the dog curiously.

The animal sat by the bale, and Janine returned her

attention to the stall where Shannon Collins was helping the mare through her labor.

"Does she know what she's doing?" Rafe asked Cora, intrigued by Shannon in spite of himself.

"That girl *always* knows what she's doing." The assurance in Cora's voice didn't allay Rafe's anxiety where his daughter was concerned.

A horse neighed in the stall behind Rafe as if in sympathy with what the mare was going through.

Shannon crossed to where Rafe was standing. He again caught that sweet scent and wondered if Shannon's perfume was something very simple or something elaborate that cost as much as Nancy's perfumes used to.

Before he had time to get enmeshed in thoughts of his wife and the guilt that went with them, Shannon was speaking to his daughter. "I'll bet you're wondering if the mare's hurting. She is a little because her baby—her foal—is moving through the birth canal inside of her. He or she grew in there for eleven months."

Janine's eyes grew wide.

"That *is* a long time," Shannon agreed, as if Janine had said as much. "If you watch very closely when the foal begins to be born, you'll see the front feet first and then the nose. But you won't see them clearly because they're in a sac—sort of like a big clear balloon—that has protected him or her. Once the foal's nose is out, the rest will happen fast, and Dancer will break the sac and lick her baby. Are you sure you still want to stay?"

Janine nodded once again.

Shannon's gaze met Rafe's briefly. It was like a collision, and Rafe couldn't understand why he was reacting to this woman so strongly. He didn't react to women anymore. That's just the way it was.

Shannon looked away and motioned to Clancy. "Dancer's used to you. I think it would be all right if you want to stand outside her stall, as long as you don't make any quick movements."

Clancy's nearly black eyes had darted to Rafe now and then, and he'd seemed almost sullen. Now at Shannon's words he grinned, and Rafe saw a change in the boy. The defiance was suddenly gone as he went to the stall.

Late-afternoon sun streamed through high, hazy windows. A pane in one of them was broken. The smells of horses and hay and leather brought back memories of the times Rafe had gone riding with his wife. The stables they'd frequented were much different from this ancient barn, which he suspected had been standing for decades. He glanced over his shoulder and up into the hayloft. There he caught sight of a gray tabby with paws outstretched, sunbathing on a hay bale.

Janine suddenly moved, and he was alert as to what she was doing. She'd taken hold of the top of the stall and was putting her foot on the rung above the bale to hike herself up.

She'd been a little monkey before everything had happened, always climbing on her jungle gym, scampering up and down the ladder to her tree house. For a long time now she'd preferred to stay indoors, watch TV or just sit in her room staring out the window.

"Oh, look!" Cora murmured to Rafe almost reverently.

Rafe had never seen a foal born. He'd been present at Janine's birth, and nothing in his life had prepared him for that miracle. Though he hadn't spent much time in church, Rafe suddenly felt as if that type of hallowed atmosphere overcame everyone watching. He kept one eye on Janine, in case she was troubled by anything. But as he watched the process unfold and glanced at Shannon Collins's face alive with joy, the past eighteen months seemed to have less of a grip on him. As Shannon had explained, the front hooves of the foal appeared, covered in membrane. The head was lying on the extended forelegs. Then the shoulders appeared, and quickly the rest of the foal's body. The balloon broke and the foal kicked free from the mare.

Janine was watching raptly, as though she felt the same sense of awe that Rafe felt.

After the mare got to her feet, Shannon stepped out of the stall and came over to Janine. "That was something, wasn't it?" she asked.

Janine nodded, still wide-eyed, staring at the foal.

"In a little while Dancer will lick her and warm her up, and then this little filly will start nursing, which means she'll be taking milk from her mother."

At the mention of the word *mother,* Rafe watched his daughter's face. There wasn't a flicker that she was thinking of anything other than the horse and the foal. Still, he wanted to make something clear to Shannon Collins right now. "Does the horse need you?"

She looked up at him with some surprise. "No. I thought Janine might like to watch for a while longer."

"She can watch," Rafe responded, "but I'd like a word with you."

Cora spoke up then and nodded to the golden retriever. "Buster and Clancy want to see the little filly drink for the first time. We're going to stay right here if you two want to go into the tack room.''

Rafe could see an open door to a room across the barn where saddles hung on pegs along the wall. "That would be fine." He clasped his daughter's shoulder. "I'm going to be right over there with Dr. Collins."

Janine just gave the half shrug he was used to, that said she'd heard but she didn't really care.

With a frown he crossed the barn and waited for Janine's new therapist to join him.

Shannon's day had taken off like a runaway horse. She'd intended to be finished not only with clients, but also with chores when Rafe Pierson and his daughter arrived. Then Dancer had gone into labor, and there were plenty of chores still left undone. When Rafe Pierson had appeared...

The impact of meeting his gaze for the first time had unsettled her. The *man* unsettled her. It had been years since any man had done that. The problem was—this unsettling was made up of a combination of things. He was definitely a man used to being in control, yet she could see how gentle and concerned he was with his daughter. There was something terrifically and powerfully male about him that had taken her unawares. Right now she knew they had a confrontation coming. He hadn't liked the way she'd handled Janine. That had been all too obvious.

Once they were inside the tack room, Shannon shut the door. When she did, Rafe Pierson's shoulders in his tan polo shirt seemed much too wide, and his khaki slacks seemed to fit him much too...casually. She could tell how fit he was just by looking at him. A thrill of attraction skittered through her. She couldn't remember a man ever making her feel this excited and kind of quivery inside.

"Dr. Collins, I think you should be aware—"

"It's Shannon."

He stopped as if he hadn't expected her to interrupt him. "All right...Shannon. I think we should get something straight. *I* know what Janine's been through. I've lived through it with her. Although you'll be treating her, I'm still her father, and I make the decisions about her welfare."

Although he'd lit a fuse to Shannon's temper, she kept a lid on it. "You're her father, Mr. Pierson, but I'm going to be her therapist. I thought I'd made it clear when we talked that this therapy isn't about a limited session each day. It's going to involve every interaction I have with Janine and how she reacts to everyone here as well as the horses. There's no beginning and end to a session. Her therapy started when you walked through that barn door, and it'll end when you leave the Rocky R."

Rafe's very defined jaw tightened. "When I agreed to stay here, I didn't agree to give you unilateral control over my daughter."

"What did you agree to?" she asked softly.

He raked his hand through his hair. "I agreed to let you try to help her where nobody else could. You said you needed me here, too, and I assumed that was to take care of her."

Shannon had gone through Janine's case history at least three times, including every therapist's note, every medical doctor's observations, everything she could possibly glean from reading between the lines, as well as what was on the typed pages. "How do you feel Janine reacted to watching Dancer give birth?"

"She seemed entranced," he said tersely.

"Do you think it upset her in any way?"

"No," he admitted as if it was hard to do.

"The decision was Janine's to make and she had to know that. She has to know that she has some power over her life. I tried to give her some. This therapy is only going to work, Mr. Pierson, if you trust me."

His shoulders squared. "How am I supposed to do that when I don't even know you?"

His question seemed to reverberate in the small room, and Shannon realized she might have to get to know Rafe Pierson as well as Janine, in order to help the little girl. "You knew my credentials before you called me. Now you're going to have to give me a chance."

When he remained silent, she went on. "This type of therapy isn't for everyone. If you're having second thoughts—"

"Second, third and fourth thoughts," he cut in. "I don't like being backed into a corner. This whole situation has done that to us, because you're the only corner we have left right now. As far as trusting you, I'll trust you when I see results. I'll trust you when I know that what you're doing is working."

Apparently he was used to dealing in blunt honesty. She'd have to be just as honest. "We have to cooperate or this therapy *won't* work."

The air was heavy with the tension that had sprung up between them. After interminable moments he broke it. "Fine. We'll cooperate. But I have final say in what's best for my daughter."

"I think Janine will have final say in what's best for her."

He stared at Shannon as if she'd suddenly sprouted

a second nose. Still, she knew the key to unlocking Janine was Janine. She also knew that this man, who did his best to control the courtroom, had to have some control here, too. "Do you think your daughter's ready to get settled in at the house now?"

He gave her a wry smile. "You're good, Dr. Collins. Just don't forget, I know how to handle people, too."

That sounded too much like a warning. Instead of bristling, she raised her chin, opened the door and then reminded him, "It's Shannon."

A half hour later Shannon watched Rafe remove luggage from his trunk and set it on the ground. The large black suitcase and traveling bag were apparently his, the smaller pink-and-white-striped one his daughter's. Shannon was still trying to get a fix on the man and her reaction to him. He was obviously worried about his daughter. But Shannon sensed something else about Rafe. She suspected he'd concentrated on Janine since her mother's death, and possibly ignored some of his own deepest feelings. She guessed he particularly hadn't faced his anger about what had happened to his wife and to his daughter.

Even after all these years, Shannon was still wary of angry men…because of her father. She knew how to deal with a gamut of emotions in children, including anger, but in adults she automatically backed away from it. Yet, something about Rafe Pierson made everything inside of her stand up and take notice. She was going to have to be careful she didn't become overly involved with this father as well as his daughter. It had been two years since she'd bought the Rocky R, suffered a broken engagement and decided her work was all she needed for a fulfilling life...without a man. She couldn't imagine ever changing her mind.

Janine had pulled a canvas tote bag out of the trunk and didn't stray far from her father's side. Buster plopped down beside her again and looked up at her adoringly.

Shannon noticed the flicker of interest in the little girl's eyes and was relieved by it. Janine might have stopped talking, but she hadn't cut herself off from the world. Shannon picked up Janine's suitcase.

Before she took a step, Rafe offered, "I can come back for that one."

"No need," Shannon decided. "I'm a lot stronger than I look."

When his gaze swept over her appraisingly, she felt hotter than if she'd spent the afternoon in the sun. An appreciative expression that flickered momentarily on Rafe's face told her he might feel the same sparks she did.

Shannon led the parade to the house and stopped momentarily in the living room. It wasn't customary for clients to enter her house. Her office was in the renovated bunkhouse. Looking around at the comfortable, overstuffed coral-and-blue couch, the light pine tables and entertainment center, the large cross-stitched sampler her aunt had made for her that hung above the sofa, Shannon tried to see it through Rafe's eyes.

"Feel free to use the TV and stereo whenever you'd like."

"Do you often have clients stay with you?" Rafe asked, his gaze dark and intense.

"No. Just now and then, when I think it's necessary.

You live so far from here, I didn't see any other way to handle Janine's therapy.''

"You're a brave woman, having strangers in your house.''

"Just as you've checked my credentials, I've checked you out, too.'' She motioned to the back of the living room. "My bedroom is down that hall. You and Janine will be sleeping upstairs.''

A rattling of pots and pans came from the kitchen. "Aunt Cora will be cooking most of the meals.'' Shannon looked directly at Janine. "If there's anything you really like to eat, you'll have to let her know.''

Janine looked panicked for a moment, but Shannon was quick to reassure her, "You can write it down or draw a picture.''

Buster's blond tail whished back and forth as Shannon led the way to the stairs and climbed them swiftly.

As he mounted the steps, Rafe asked, "Your aunt Cora lives here, too?''

"She has her own apartment in the bunkhouse. She's my office manager and she keeps the house running smoothly. That way I can concentrate on the ranch and my clients.''

"In that order?''

She stopped in the hall to wait for Janine and returned lightly, "I've heard that attorneys ask a lot of questions. Now I know it's true.''

The nerve in Rafe's jaw worked, and Shannon didn't know why he was getting under her skin. She'd have to ignore her own reactions and concentrate on making Janine feel at home.

Pointing to a switch on the wall, she said, "This turns on the ceiling fan.'' She nodded to the wooden fan set above the staircase landing. "Especially at night, it will help keep the rooms cooler up here."

Continuing to the first room on the right, Shannon took Janine's suitcase to the bed, laid it on top of the patchwork quilt and said to the seven-year-old, "This will be your room while you're here. You can put anything anyplace you want, come up here anytime you want. Your dad's going to be right next door. If you need him and he's over there, you don't even have to go get him. You can just knock on the wall and he'll hear you."

Buster had followed Shannon into the room, and now he hopped up onto the bed. "If you want Buster to stay here with you, he can. If not, I'll take him with me."

Janine gave a little shrug and went over to the window and looked out.

"I'll help her get settled in," Rafe said.

"That's fine. I'm sure you'd both like to rest or freshen up after your drive. I'm going back out to the barn for a while. Either Cora or I will let you know when supper's ready."

While Rafe took his suitcases next door, Janine left the window and went over to the bed, hopping up onto it beside the dog. Buster turned and rested his nose on her leg. Janine laid her hand on his head, and Shannon almost smiled.

After she told Janine she'd see her later, she went down to the kitchen.

Cora was forming ground beef patties on a saucer. "I thought I'd make chopped-steak burgers and mashed potatoes for tonight. What do you think?"

"That's fine."

Cora looked at her niece. "It's going to be an interesting summer, isn't it?"

"I don't know what you mean."

"Oh, girl, you sure *do* know what I mean. Firecrackers are poppin' between you and Mr. Pierson."

"And that means?" Shannon asked.

"It means—you know he's a man and he knows you're a woman."

At that Shannon laughed. "You've got a great imagination."

"I sure do, and I use it as often as I can. By the way, Nolan called while you were outside."

Nolan Constantine had seemed to want to get to know Shannon better and had taken her out to dinner a few times. But she wasn't interested in being more than friends. She'd told him that after their last date when he'd tried to kiss her. "Did he say what he wanted?"

"Just said to give you the message he'd be stoppin' by later."

A buzzer went off in the laundry room beyond the kitchen. "Are those the towels?" Shannon asked.

"Yep. Do you want me to take them up to our guests?"

"No, I'll do it before I go out to the barn."

Shannon pulled two sets of fresh peach towels from the dryer and folded them, then carried them upstairs. When she stopped at Janine's room, the door was still open, but the little girl had fallen asleep with Buster beside her on the bed.

Shannon laid one set of towels on the chair inside the door, then tiptoed out without waking her new client.

Rafe's door was partially open. She decided not to

disturb him. She'd simply put the towels in the bathroom...

Suddenly he pulled his door wide open on his way out of the room.

The towels slipped from Shannon's hands. Rafe Pierson was naked from the waist up, and black curling hair furred his chest. His skin was tanned and taut, and when she finally lifted her gaze to his green eyes, she couldn't speak. Rafe Pierson was absolutely the most sexy man she'd ever seen.

Chapter Two

Heat rushed to Shannon's cheeks. She felt like a total idiot with the towels at her feet.

She never responded to men this way. Never.

Tearing her gaze from Rafe, she bent to pick up the towels. He stooped at the same time she did, bringing their faces very close.

"I was going to wash up." His voice was deep and husky, rasping against her already jarred nerve endings. He smelled musky and male, and she could picture him at the sink. She could picture him— She straightened quickly, banishing the images.

He came up more slowly than she did, a washcloth in his hand.

She stuffed a bath towel and hand towel into his arms. "You'll...you'll need these. I put Janine's on the chair in her room. She fell asleep."

"She did?" He seemed surprised at that, and he

walked over to the room and peeked inside. When he turned back into the hall, he said, "She seems to have a bodyguard. Is he safe with kids? I mean—"

"Buster's great with kids. He's obviously taken a liking to her." Again Shannon's gaze slid to the hair on Rafe's chest.

"I understand your clients are mostly children."

She didn't know if he was making conversation for the heck of it or if he wanted to know more about her. Apparently *he* was comfortable being half-naked, even though his bare chest was making her thoughts scatter. "Children make up the majority of my practice."

Then he cocked his head, studying her even more completely. "Why did you become a psychologist?"

Everything in her stilled, and his green eyes seemed too perceptive. "That's a long story."

He arched a brow. "And a private one?"

"Yes."

"But you can sum it up," he persisted.

Along with the interest, challenge sparked in Rafe's green eyes. He was daring her to reveal something about herself. After all, she knew quite a bit about him and Janine, and he only had professional knowledge of her. "I was afraid a lot as a child. Overcoming my fears was difficult. But I did, and I want to help other children do that, too."

There was silence for a few moments as he absorbed her answer. "How long have you been practicing here—at the Rocky R?"

"I bought the ranch two years ago. I had a mentor when I was in college who used horses in her therapy. I saw what a difference they made. After I earned my Ph.D. and was practicing, I had some pretty tough cases. A lot of the clients I see have nothing to do with the horses. More and more do. I'd like to build up a reputation in that area so I can help more children that way.''

''I still don't completely understand it,'' he admitted.

She admired his honesty. ''You will.''

''Shannon?'' her Aunt Cora called from the foot of the stairs. ''Clancy needs to talk to you.''

Taking advantage of the summons, she moved toward the stairs. ''I'll see you at supper.''

Then, before her gaze dropped to the hair on Rafe Pierson's chest again, before it swept down to his belt buckle, she hurried to her aunt, trying to forget how this deputy district attorney from Salinas affected her.

Cora kept up a lively conversation with Rafe during dinner, while Shannon tried to make Janine feel at home. Every now and then her gaze would connect with Rafe's, and she remembered how he'd looked without his shirt. It was much easier to concentrate on his daughter.

After dinner Shannon was walking to the barn with Rafe and Janine to see the new foal when Nolan Constantine's white Cadillac rolled down the lane. He parked and met Shannon on the walk in front of the house.

Nolan was blond and blue-eyed, owned a computer store in Fawn Grove as well as another in Palermo and had a smile that should have melted Shannon in her boots. Yet it never had. He was the most eligible bachelor in Fawn Grove, and probably the wealthiest, but Shannon simply didn't care about that. Her one attempt at a serious relationship had ended soon after she'd bought the Rocky R...partially *because* of her buying the Rocky R. She'd been hurt when her fiancé had called off their engagement, though not as hurt as she would have been if she'd ended up in a marriage with him. He'd wanted to control too much about her life.

She wasn't sure any man could love her simply as she was, without the need to have the final say on what she did and how she did it. She'd come too far for that. Turning thirty-one in a few months, she was well aware of her biological clock ticking, and she wanted to be a mother. In a way she mothered all of her clients. At least once a week she told herself she had options—artificial insemination and single-parent adoption among them. Although she was in debt, she was doing well and she knew she could swing expenses for an adoption. But she'd have to put her dream for an indoor riding ring on hold if she adopted a child.

As Nolan strode across the grass in his designer suit and shiny loafers, Shannon saw Rafe sizing up the man. She also noticed how Janine hung back from all of them, keeping her distance from the stranger.

Shannon introduced the two men and went over to Janine, explaining that Nolan was a friend.

But Rafe was suddenly beside his daughter, dropping his arm around her shoulders. "I'll take her down to the barn."

Janine tugged on her dad's hand, and Shannon guessed that she was anxious to see the foal again.

As Shannon stared after Rafe's broad back, Nolan asked, "You have guests?"

"Mr. Pierson and his daughter are from Salinas. They're staying here while I start Janine's therapy."

Nolan's brows raised. "He must have a crackerjack job or be self-employed to be able to take time off."

Shannon didn't discuss her clients, and Nolan should realize that. "What brings you out here tonight?"

"Even though you're treating his daughter, Mr. Pierson comes under your confidentiality clause, too?" Nolan asked with a wry smile.

"That's right."

Giving a shrug as if it didn't matter, Nolan answered her question. "I came for a visit. I haven't seen you for a while."

"It's only been two weeks," she teased, trying to overcome the remnants of tension left from their last date.

"When we had dinner, things ended kind of awkwardly," Nolan admitted honestly. "I wanted to make sure you knew I wasn't going to push anything. You're single. I'm single. There's no reason why we can't just enjoy each other's company now and then."

Nolan was the ultimate diplomat. He'd make a great politician with his easy smile and facile handling of every situation. Still, in his eyes she saw more than just a desire for friendship. Her radar where men were concerned was usually on the mark. She'd honed her intuition as a child until she'd trusted it implicitly. She'd had to, to keep herself safe.

And it had worked...until that one night.

Forgetting was so much harder than moving on. Some moments could never be erased.

"Besides straightening all of that out, there *is* something else I want to talk to you about," Nolan added.

"Why don't we go inside? Aunt Cora made a pitcher of lemonade."

Until Shannon poured Nolan lemonade and offered him a piece of the coconut cake Cora had made for dessert, they engaged in further small talk about the happenings in Fawn Grove and concert presentations in Sacramento for the summer. They *did* have a lot of interests in common, but not enough. Certainly not the sizzle she felt whenever she looked at Rafe Pierson.

Since when had she ever been concerned about sizzle? In a way sizzle scared her. It was so foreign she wasn't sure how to handle it.

She and Nolan were seated on the couch in the living room. He'd removed his suitcoat and tugged down his tie as he told her about a seventy-year-old male customer who wanted one of those "new-fangled machines" that could help him find a lady friend longdistance. Apparently he'd heard about chat rooms.

Nolan knew how to tell a story. Shannon was still laughing about Nolan's customer, who was ready to make his mark on the Internet dating scene, when Nolan's expression turned serious. "Enough about my business for one night. I came out here to discuss yours."

"You mean my practice?" she asked, curious in spite of herself.

"Sort of. Are you still thinking about building that indoor ring?" Nolan picked up his glass of lemonade and took a few swallows.

"I think it's going to be a while until I can accomplish that."

He returned his glass to the coaster on the coffee table. "But you still want it?"

Want it? It was one of those dreams it might take a lifetime to fulfill. "Oh, yes. If I had the ring inside, I could have classes no matter what the weather. I could gear my practice mainly toward equine therapy.''

When he shifted toward her, his expression was earnest. "Then I want you to think about something. I have a business proposition for you. I'll give you a substantial donation for the indoor ring if you'll let me have a news crew here when I present the money to you."

Shannon was stunned. "You can't be serious!"

"I'm very serious. I don't joke about money."

She studied him carefully. "But why would you want to do that?"

"Two reasons," he responded quickly, as if he'd been prepared for her question. "It'll be a write-off for me, and I can certainly use that. I also want the publicity. I'm opening a third store in Sacramento, and I have a contact at the TV station there. I'm sure I can get a news crew out here. It would be great for your practice, too…help get the word out on what you do."

"I still don't understand, Nolan. You can buy advertising time."

"That would probably cost more than this donation," he insisted with one of his convincing smiles. "Besides, this kind of thing— People like it. If they think I'm a great guy, then they're likely to do business with me."

She smiled at his unabashed honesty.

Before they could discuss the idea further, the front screen door opened, and Rafe, Janine and Cora came inside with Buster at Janine's heels.

Rafe took in the two glasses of lemonade, Nolan's empty dish, his tugged-down tie. "Sorry. We didn't mean to interrupt. I thought we could watch TV for a little while before Janine went to bed."

Nolan rose to his feet and picked up his suitcoat. "I've got to get home, anyway. I have a few calls to make. Shannon, walk me to my car?"

It didn't seem possible, but already Shannon could sense the two men didn't like each other. She had told Rafe that he and Janine could have the run of the house. Entertaining a visitor wasn't a usual occurrence for her.

Rising to her feet, she played the gracious hostess. Avoiding Rafe's gaze, she motioned to the remote on the coffee table. "Go ahead." Then she went over to Janine and crouched down in front of her. "Would you like Buster to sleep with you tonight?"

Janine glanced up at Cora.

"That's fine with me," the older lady said. "Sometimes his tail thumping on the floor keeps me awake."

Shannon thought she saw Janine's lips twitch slightly, as if she wanted to smile. Then she was serious again and just nodded at Shannon that she'd like Buster to stay with her.

Nolan crossed to the door, and as Shannon started to do the same, Janine caught her hand and then squeezed it. Shannon gazed into the little girl's eyes and could see it was a thank-you squeeze. It was also a very big, first step in reaching out.

Emotion choked Shannon's throat for a moment, and she took Janine's hand in both of hers. "You're welcome."

Janine pulled away from her then, but important first contact had been made.

Shannon could feel Rafe's gaze on her as she went outside with Nolan.

When Shannon returned from walking Nolan to his car, Rafe was standing on the porch, his hands on the railing, as he looked up into the mysteries of the black night. Glancing inside, Shannon could see Janine lying on the sofa watching TV, Buster beside her on the floor.

"Your aunt said to tell you she was turning in," Rafe said with a nod toward the bunkhouse.

"I saw her going over there."

"I guess she thought you might be too tied up to notice."

Shannon wasn't sure what to say to that. The climbing roses alongside the porch scented the warm night. Rafe was wearing a black T-shirt and blue jeans and looked less like a prosecuting attorney than a rebel who should be driving a hot rod. Her heart had started beating faster as soon as she'd caught a glimpse of him, and now as he turned away from the sky toward her, it practically stopped.

"Do you and Constantine have something going?" he asked casually.

The question ruffled her, and she wasn't exactly sure why. "Look, Mr. Pierson. Just because you and your daughter are staying here doesn't mean—"

"It's Rafe," he interrupted, looking down at her with an intensity that made her want to take several deep breaths.

"Rafe," she repeated, and it sounded much too intimate coming from her lips.

He rested one hand on the porch post above her head. "I don't have any right to know anything about your business, but I'm just curious. I overheard his proposition."

"You were eavesdropping!"

"No. I was waiting on the porch for Cora and Janine to catch up. Constantine's voice carries. Are you going to accept his offer?''

"I told him I'd think about it.''

Rafe's voice went deeper. "You'd better think long and hard. I'm sure there are strings attached.''

"If you were listening, then you know that there are. Nolan wants the publicity. It's that simple.''

Rafe narrowed his eyes. "To sell a few more computers? That doesn't wash with me.''

"It doesn't have to. It isn't any of your concern.''

Rafe's body was very close to hers, and she felt a quickening...a restless yearning that she'd never experienced before. Needing to make her getaway, she moved a step toward the door. "I'm going to say good-night to Janine and then turn in. I'll be working with her first thing in the morning after chores. Is there anything else you need?''

The moon illuminated one side of Rafe's angular face, and she thought she saw longing there, as well as a deep need she couldn't begin to meet.

After a few long silent moments, he shook his head. "No. We'll be fine. I'll make sure I lock the door after I come in.''

Considering his profession, she guessed he *would* make sure of something like that. Leaving him at the railing, she crossed the wooden porch, opened the screen door and stepped over the threshold. Dealing with Rafe was going to be as complicated as helping his daughter. She'd better prepare herself for that...and prepare well.

Usually Shannon was tired enough after a day working with clients, horses and chores that she fell right to sleep. But tonight...

She thought of Nolan's offer and what an indoor ring would mean to her practice. She thought about the new foal and the look in Janine's eyes as she'd watched it come into the world. She thought about the look on Rafe's face whenever he gazed at his daughter, and the deep green intensity there when he looked at Shannon.

After trying to read, she switched on the radio to let music lull her to sleep. She dozed off for a while, but when she awoke again and checked the clock, it was 1:00 a.m. Maybe what she needed was a piece of Aunt Cora's cake. She'd bypassed it at supper and again when she'd cut a piece for Nolan. Sometimes a girl just needed comfort food, and now seemed to be one of those times. Along with a tall glass of milk it might help her put everything in perspective.

Her curly hair lay tumbled and loose on her shoulders as she went down the short hall, through the living room, toward the light in the kitchen. There was a small fluorescent light over the kitchen sink that she always left turned on at night.

But when she reached the kitchen, she froze. Rafe was at the counter slicing himself a piece of cake. He was wearing a faded T-shirt, and his sleeping shorts rode low on his hips. His legs were terrifically long, his feet masculine and as bare as hers.

His gaze passed over her, and hers passed over him. Her sleep shirt came to her knees, and it was heavy enough not to be revealing. Still, she felt naked.

"We must have had the same idea," he noted, breaking the silence first. "The cake is great. Interested?"

She was finding herself much too interested in more

than the cake. "Yes. Would you like milk to go with it?"

"I wouldn't have it any other way," he answered with a boyish look that made her smile.

He found forks while she poured milk. Then they moved to the large maple table, and he pulled out the chair at the head. Her smile faded as she thought about going to the other end to keep a good bit of distance between them, but knew that would be foolish.

Picking up her glass, she sat across the corner from Rafe and took a bite of her cake, glancing at him, but he didn't look back. He seemed to have something on his mind. They didn't talk as they ate, and the quiet wasn't comfortable. Shannon couldn't think of a thing to say for the life of her. Her intuition told her Rafe Pierson had something to say to her, though, and she waited.

Finally he finished the slice of cake and laid down his fork. "How long do you think it will be before you know whether or not you're making any progress with Janine?"

In her conversation with Rafe on the phone, she'd told him there was no way to determine how long therapy might take. Then she remembered Janine reaching for her hand earlier in the evening. "In about a week I should be able to tell how she's responding to me and the horses, and life here in general. As I told you, there's no way to determine how long this is going to take. You said you can be here until August fifth. If it takes longer than that, you can go back to Salinas, and Janine can stay here with me. But we've discussed all this. Has something changed? Must you get back sooner?"

He pushed his plate away. "No. I don't need to go

back sooner. In fact…I need time away as much as Janine needs therapy that works.''

Shannon found herself interested, and not simply because of treating Rafe's daughter. ''Are you thinking of not returning to your position?''

''I'm thinking—and rethinking—everything.''

There was something troubling about Rafe's words, and she wanted to help him. Not because she was a therapist, but because she felt so drawn to him. ''I know Janine's mother was killed in a fast-food restaurant, and your daughter saw the whole thing. Do you feel responsible because you weren't there with them?'' It was called survivor guilt, and Shannon had seen it before.

He propped his forearm on the table and ran his hand through his hair. When he looked back at her, her breath almost caught from the depth of the turmoil there. ''I feel responsible, because I *was* responsible.''

''You couldn't have been responsible,'' she argued reasonably.

''You mean because I didn't pull the trigger? I might as well have. It was *my* fault. George Fulton went after Nancy to get revenge on *me*.'' Rafe's voice had gone deep and raspy with the admission.

Everything in Shannon stilled. She'd thought the shooting had been random, a madman who'd gone off the deep end. ''Because of your work?''

''Hell, yes, because of my work!'' Rafe's chair scraped the linoleum as he pushed it back and stood. ''I sent George Fulton's younger brother to prison for murder. He was twenty, in and out of trouble as a teenager. But Fulton insisted his kid brother was innocent. He wasn't. I proved to a jury he wasn't. Craig got a life sentence and his brother was furious.''

Rafe paced back and forth across the kitchen as he spoke. "I'm not popular with the bad guys, Shannon. I know that. It goes with the territory. But sometimes fate compounds fury, taking it into the realm of madness."

"What happened?" she asked softly, to encourage him to go on. From the way his words had tumbled out, she doubted if he'd ever let these feelings loose to anyone.

"Craig was killed in prison, and his brother blamed me."

"Oh, Rafe." She stood too, then, not able to bear what he was going through, wanting to comfort him somehow.

It was as if Rafe needed to get it out, to explain so Shannon could really help his daughter. "Fulton found out where I lived and followed Nancy. After he shot her, he got into a gunfight with the police. Before he died, he told them that he wanted to take away somebody I loved, the same way I'd taken away his brother."

"But you didn't!"

"I don't have to be crazy to see it like he did, Shannon. If I hadn't sent his brother to prison, Craig would be alive."

"You had no choice."

When Rafe stopped pacing, he stared at her. "That's right. My job gave me no choice. Before Nancy got killed, I almost had everything I ever wanted in my grasp. Then in a blink of an eye, it was all gone."

She couldn't help going to him...touching his arm. "You still have Janine."

"Do I?" he asked in a low voice. "She blames me,

too. I can see it in her eyes. That's why she won't talk to me. That's why she won't talk to anyone.''

Maybe Janine blamed her father, but maybe she didn't. Shannon couldn't tell Rafe his reasoning wasn't correct, though she suspected there was a lot more to Janine's silence than that.

Shannon dropped her hand from his arm because his skin electrified her. There was too much heat and too much intensity. She'd be a fool to get involved with Rafe Pierson.

''You are *not* responsible for what a criminal did,'' she insisted. Though true, her words seemed like a platitude even to her.

''I tell myself that every day. It doesn't help.''

The nerve in his jaw worked, and she had the impulsive desire to touch it…to soothe it. ''What will help?'' she asked.

She saw the answer in his eyes—the means a man uses to forget, even if only for a few moments.

In the hush of the kitchen, there was an aura of sensual awareness between them. The dim light caught the gray strands at Rafe's temples, emphasized the raven blackness of the rest. The character lines around his eyes were deep now, the stubble of his beard a shadow on his strong jaw. She could feel the beat of her heart pounding in a unified rhythm with his. She couldn't see his pulse beating, but she could sense it.

Time stopped. The dark of night promised forbidden pleasures…dangerous entanglement…a journey to somewhere she'd never been before. She could help Rafe forget and she could give herself a memory that she knew would last a lifetime.

Yet if she did, she wouldn't be helping him, and *she'd* have more regrets than she could live with.

As Rafe bent his head to take whatever she could give, she backed away, realizing how very dangerous it was going to be having Rafe under the same roof. "I can't get involved with you."

"I'm not your client," he snapped, and along with the consternation on his face she could see he was sorry he'd told her everything.

"No, you're not."

He backed away from her, too. "It would have just been a kiss, Shannon. No big deal."

It *would* have been a very big deal for her. Feeling defensive, she murmured, "That's a good enough reason not to even *think* about doing it."

The twist of his mouth was cynical. "Are you telling me you believe in stars exploding and the earth moving?"

She couldn't keep looking into his eyes, feeling the pull toward him. Turning away, she busily took the dishes from the table and carried them over to the sink. If she told him she believed in a love she'd never felt, in a tenderness she'd never experienced, in a chemistry she could hardly imagine, he'd think she was a fool. Maybe she was.

Hearing him move behind her, she still wasn't prepared when his arm almost brushed hers as he set the glasses beside the dishes in the sink. "I didn't think there were any dreamers still left in this world."

When she looked up at him, she wondered what kind of marriage he'd had...if consuming love had been part of it...if he was as grief-stricken as he was troubled about everything that had happened. But those were answers it might be better not having.

"Only a dreamer could have envisioned this ranch and the help I might be able to offer children, so don't dismiss dreamers so lightly.'' Needing to breathe in air somewhere Rafe wasn't, she informed him, ''I have a long day scheduled tomorrow. I'll see you at breakfast.'' Then she started for her room.

This time Rafe caught her shoulder. The heat of his fingers seeped through the cotton of her nightshirt. ''I may not be fully convinced that the therapy you do works, but I sincerely *hope* it does.''

Then he released her, and for the first time in her career, she didn't just hope she could succeed—she knew she had to.

Chapter Three

An early riser even when he tossed and turned all night, Rafe showered and dressed, looked in on Janine, who was still sleeping soundly, and noticed Buster was no longer by her side. When he went downstairs to the kitchen, he was relieved to see Cora rather than Shannon scrambling eggs in a large bowl.

He didn't know what had gotten into him last night. He'd spilled his guts to a woman he'd almost kissed. That wasn't like him. He didn't know what it was about Shannon Collins that got to him. He'd dealt with psychologists and psychiatrists as witnesses over the years, most of them competent. They knew how to listen well, and many of them were superiorly trained at handling people and situations. With Shannon he sensed a genuine sincerity that had nothing to do with her profession. He also saw a quickening in her dark-brown eyes that seemed to act as tinder to the low fire burning inside him whenever he got near her.

It was crazy. He knew better than to believe a one-night escape between the sheets with Dr. Collins would alleviate his guilt or drive out his worry about Janine.

Cora put down the dish of eggs, looked up and saw Rafe standing in the doorway. "Good morning. Ready for breakfast?"

"Sounds good. Should I wake Janine?"

"I don't know what Shannon has planned for her today, but I suspect she'll be in shortly."

"She's out?"

"She was in the barn with Buster before the sun came up."

"I didn't hear her leave the house."

"She probably used the back door down by her room. No grass grows under that girl's feet. After she fed the horses, she probably spent some time with that new filly."

Cora motioned to the coffeepot. "Help yourself if you want a mug before we get breakfast going. But I warn you, I make it strong."

He smiled at that. "That's the way I like it."

"That's good to hear. Shannon dumps sugar into it. She says it's the only way she can get it down."

As he poured himself a mug of the almost-pitch-black coffee, he decided to pursue something that had been bothering him since last night. "That man who was here last evening. Are he and Shannon involved?"

Cora gave Rafe a speculative look. "That depends what you mean by 'involved.' I'm not telling any tales if I say they've been out to dinner a few times. The truth is, I think Nolan's got more on his mind than dinner.''

That had been Rafe's impression, too. "And Shannon?''

Cora just shrugged. ''I'm not so sure what she's thinkin' or feelin' about Nolan. I do know if she married him, she'd be secure for the rest of her life and wouldn't have to work as hard as she does, either. But she's so dad-blasted independent. She'll probably never marry anyone.''

Rafe had come up against that independent streak a few times, and he'd been here less than a day. He wondered what had bred it.

He caught a flash of movement outside and went over to the window to get a better look. Shannon was dressed in a blue-and-white-checked blouse and jeans today. She was coming across the lane, leading a small butter-colored Shetland pony, followed by Buster. As he watched, she unhooked the rope from the pony's halter and just left him in the front yard! Wouldn't the pony wander off? Get into something he shouldn't?

Apparently not. The animal grazed as Shannon came into the house.

She stopped when she saw Rafe in the kitchen. ''Is Janine up yet?'' she asked, her gaze avoiding his as she went to the refrigerator.

''Are you ready to work with her?''

Shannon poured herself a glass of orange juice. ''I think it would be a good idea if we all ate breakfast together. Then we'll start the real work.''

''I'll wake her.'' The sight of Shannon this morning didn't affect him any less than it had last night. She was damn attractive to him, and he was beginning to wish she was older and built like a tank.

Rafe awakened Janine and helped her get ready for her first day with Shannon. By then Cora had breakfast on the table. Throughout breakfast Shannon didn't avoid Rafe's gaze, but when she did look at him, it wasn't for very long. As they cleaned off the table and accidentally bumped into each other at the sink, she shied away from him. He realized he didn't want that.

After breakfast Rafe noticed Buster was at Janine's side again. His daughter had crouched down on the kitchen floor and was petting him when Shannon said to her, "Let's go out in the front yard. There's somebody I want you to meet."

Instantly on alert, Rafe knew this was it. This was the beginning of therapy. Even though that was a pony out there, Janine was less than a third of its size. Whether he was being protective or not, he was going to make sure no more harm came to his daughter.

Once outside, Shannon let Janine keep her distance from the pony. "Janine, this is Marigold, and she's very friendly."

The pony rubbed her head against Shannon's arm.

"See? She gets kind of lonely. She's older than the other horses and can't run and play anymore like they do. She has her own little corral and shed over there."

Pointing toward the far side of the barn, Shannon added, "She and Buster have become good friends, though. So if you want to know anything about her, ask him. And if you'd like to get to know *her* better, just look into her eyes and she'll understand you want to be her friend, too."

Shannon's explanation and smile made all of it sound very reasonable, as if communicating with horses and dogs was a natural occurrence of everyday life. Still, as Janine moved closer to the pony, Rafe did, too.

His daughter stood about a foot away from Marigold, staring at her.

The pony's ears pricked forward. Her eyes seemed brighter as her tail swished softly.

Unobtrusively, Shannon moved to Rafe's elbow. She tugged on him slightly to pull him away from his daughter and Marigold. "Let's go into the house," she suggested.

"Not on your life."

"Rafe, Marigold is twenty-six years old and as tame as a kitten. She won't hurt Janine."

"She could step on her."

Shannon spoke softly so Janine couldn't hear. "This therapy is about Janine interacting with the animals. She can't do that if you're guarding her. You have to back off and give her some space."

His voice was low but vehement. "You don't seem to get it, Shannon. I failed to protect my wife and daughter once. I won't fail to protect Janine again."

"Do you think I would do *anything*—anything at all—to put her in danger? Knowing what she's been through?"

That sincerity in Shannon's eyes pulled on an invisible cord inside of him that was wound too tight. Searching Shannon's face, he wanted to believe she knew exactly what she was doing and that Janine would be safe in her care. But he didn't trust anyone with his daughter now. Not anyone. "I'll give her space, but not so much that I can't get to her if she needs me."

Shannon's expression was troubled. "Stay far enough away that she can forget you're there. Remember, I'll be watching her, too. That's what this is all about.''

Then Janine's therapist left him in the front yard with the sun beating down on him.

After supper that evening Rafe decided he'd just be in the way while Cora and Janine baked cookies so he went for a jog along the country roads. Shannon had spent most of the day with Janine in one fashion or another, including two sessions in her office. Rafe had felt shut out then and didn't like the feeling. It was odd. When he'd taken Janine to the other therapists, he'd left her there hoping they could solve the problem. Here, with Shannon Collins, it was different. He didn't know why.

He cooled down by walking the Rocky R's lane and heading for the barn. The old building drew him, and he realized he didn't miss the city at all. Or his career. Maybe he'd carried the banner for justice too long. Maybe he'd finally realized justice was a concept rather than a reality.

When he opened the barn door, he saw the lights were on. Then he spotted Shannon grooming a buckskin mare.

''You're working late,'' he said as he approached her.

''Sometimes the chores seem never ending,'' she admitted.

''You need permanent help.''

''Someday, maybe. Are the cookies finished yet?''

''I don't know. I went for a jog. I felt...pent-up.''

''On the Rocky R that's impossible,'' she teased with a quick smile.

That smile slammed into him like a gut punch. "I guess it's a state of mind."

As one of her hands took a brush down the horse's neck, her other ruffled the mane and Rafe wondered what it would be like to have her hands on him. Jeez, he was losing his grip.

"It'll get easier," she said, as if she knew.

"Nothing's easy anymore," he muttered.

"Some things are," she assured him. "Come here."

Curious, he took a few steps closer to her, and she handed him the grooming brush. "Take this over Cloppy's back."

He took the brush from her. "Cloppy?"

"Her first owner's son named her. That's the way she sounded when she walked."

Rafe examined the horse. "How many owners has she had?"

"Two, before me. Her first owner bought her because his son wanted a horse. Then his son lost interest in *having* a horse. Her second owner couldn't keep up the farm and had to sell all his livestock. That's how I found her."

Rafe took the brush over the mare, finding a soothing quality in doing so. "Do you use her with kids?"

"I use all the horses with kids. I selected them for that reason. Cloppy, here, is a Welsh-Arabian pony."

"She's big for a pony."

"At fourteen hands, she's considered a large pony, and she's big enough for adults to ride, too."

Though he kept smoothing his brush over the pony, Rafe's attention was on Shannon. "Have you been around horses all of your life?"

"Goodness, no," Shannon said with a shake of her head that made her curls fly.

"So when did you become interested in them?"

She seemed to hesitate, and he realized she was reluctant to tell him about herself. Why was that? Just being professional? Or hiding secrets?

After a few moments she explained, "When I was a teenager, I had a friend whose family owned a ranch. I spent as much time there as I could. I discovered that horses listened even better than people. They have this intuitive quality—" She stopped abruptly. "You probably think I'm crazy."

"Not crazy. Just different."

It took her a moment to realize he was teasing, and then she smiled at him. "Hmm. 'Different' is one way of putting it. Horses really *are* intuitive, and some of them seem downright psychic."

As he moved the brush over Cloppy's hindquarters, he gave Shannon an amused glance. "You've got to realize I've only ever *ridden* horses. I've never had a conversation with one."

"Maybe you should try it," she retorted, as she held Cloppy's halter and looked into the horse's big brown eyes. "Right, Cloppy? I'll bet you could teach Mr. Pierson just how good a best friend you could be."

"That's an old-fashioned concept." Lots of things about Shannon seemed old-fashioned—in a very satisfying way.

She looked surprised. "Having a best friend is old-fashioned?"

"Yeah. Or maybe it's just that men don't have best friends. Not in the way women do."

"I don't believe that. Wasn't your wife your best friend?"

He stopped brushing the horse.

"I'm sorry," Shannon said quickly. "I shouldn't

have asked that. I understand if you don't want to talk about—''

''It's not that I don't want to talk about it. I just never thought about my relationship with Nancy that way.'' His wife had needed him and depended on him and confided in him. She'd been blond and blue-eyed and beautiful, and the only child of older parents. It wasn't until after they were married that he realized she couldn't make decisions on her own and she needed to consult with him about everything. After Janine had been born, that had been doubly true.

From the first, Nancy had made him feel strong— as if he stood ten feet tall. As the years had passed, he'd realized that was a heavy burden, too. He had to be everything to her and provide all the solutions to their problems. It had been more like loving a child than loving a wife. Yet he *had* loved her.

''Were your parents best friends?'' he asked Shannon, wondering where she'd gotten the idea that a married couple could be. He'd never really seen a good marriage in all the foster homes he'd lived in.

''They divorced when I was nine.''

There was a quality to Shannon's voice that made him look away from the pony and directly at her.

But she turned away from him. ''That's probably enough for Cloppy for now. I guess it's getting near Janine's bedtime.''

Obviously, Shannon wanted to close the subject. He didn't particularly want to get into the subject of parents, either, so that was fine with him. ''Is there anything else you need help with?'' he asked.

As she led Cloppy to a stall, Shannon looked over her shoulder. ''You want chores to do?''

He smiled. ''Maybe I do. I'm going to have time

on my hands. Especially if you won't let me watch Janine every minute.'' He'd meant it as a joke, but it was somewhat true, too.

Shannon came out of Cloppy's stall and shut the gate. ''There's always plenty to do, from cleaning out the stalls to exercising the horses. You said you've ridden?''

''Nancy and I were weekend riders, but yes, I can hold my own on a horse. I also noticed you have downed fence along the road. I can repair that, if you'd like.''

''That's up to you. I'd be grateful, but I don't want to take advantage of you or your time.''

They were standing under the glare of a yellow lightbulb, the string floating between them. ''I get the feeling you might think attorneys are city slickers. If so, you're going to have to revise your opinion of this one. I've been around, Shannon. I've worked everything from construction sites to a judge's appointment calendar. I know the head of a nail as well as the motherboard of a computer.''

''A man of many talents,'' she joked, looking up at him, but not mocking him.

There was respect in her eyes, and he liked the feel of it. It wasn't the adoration he'd often seen in Nancy's that had weighed him down. Yet it was more than respect, too. The electricity that buzzed between them left sparks, and he could almost see them as well as feel them when he and Shannon were standing this close.

Suddenly he remembered last night and how he'd felt turned inside-out, and how his life was complicated enough. ''Just make a list of chores you'd like someone else to handle, and I'll see what I can do.''

Then he left Shannon Collins in the barn...before he kissed her...before he became reckless and forgot that pleasure was fleeting.

When Shannon came into the house a short time later, she was surprised to see Rafe in a chair in the living room reading a magazine, and Janine sitting on the stairs in her nightgown, a book on her lap, Buster at her feet.

"I thought you'd be in bed," Shannon said to the little girl, wondering what was going on.

Janine held up the book.

"I think she wants you to read to her," Rafe said, his voice deep. "She kept closing it when I tried to and then she pointed to the barn."

Shannon couldn't tell if the idea bothered him or not. "Do you want me to read you the book?" Shannon asked Janine.

Janine nodded and pointed upstairs.

They hadn't accomplished a lot in their two sessions today. Shannon had asked Janine to draw what she was thinking about, and mostly she'd drawn the horses and the foal and Buster. The surface of the river.

"I'm sure I smell like horses. I'll wash and be right up."

In her bathroom, Shannon washed her face and her hands and her arms with the honeysuckle-scented soap that she always used. Taking a quick look at her hair, she decided nothing could be done about that. The only way it was manageable was if she used a curling iron on each strand or braided it. She slid off the band on her ponytail, regathered her hair and attached it again. A little bit of tidiness would have to do. After a final glance in the mirror, she realized she'd cleaned up more for Rafe than for Janine. Troubled by the thought, she went upstairs to Janine's bedroom.

Buster had curled on the rug beside the bed, and when Shannon went into the room, Janine patted the bed next to her.

Shannon smiled, and a warm feeling overcame her. She was becoming fond of Janine, feeling the connection between them growing.

Rafe stood over by the window looking restless. When Shannon settled on the bed next to his daughter and opened the book, he lowered himself into the cane-backed rocker, his gaze on them, as if he was trying to figure something out.

Shannon read Janine a story about a dog who'd gotten separated from his family and had to find his way home. During the course of the story, Janine laid her head against Shannon's arm. Shannon's throat tightened, and she had to stop for a moment.

She'd talked to lots of children. She'd hugged them and dried their tears. She'd helped many of them overcome problems. But she'd never quite felt the amount of tenderness that she was feeling now toward Janine as the little girl's silky black hair rubbed against her arm. From what she understood, Janine had kept herself aloof from everyone for months. She wasn't aloof now, and hope gleamed even brighter in Shannon's heart that she could help this child regain her life.

By the time Shannon finished the story, she thought Janine might be asleep. But when she closed the book, the little girl looked up at her. Again she took Shannon's hand and squeezed it. That squeeze was becoming Janine's way of saying "thank you."

"You're welcome," Shannon said. "I don't often get a chance to read stories out loud. Aunt Cora's too old for them, and Buster just falls asleep.'' Shannon looked over the side of the bed at the dog. ''But I think he was listening to this one.''

That drew a smile from Janine, and Shannon wished she could take a picture of it so that Rafe could keep it and remind himself his daughter could be happy again.

Rafe stood then, and Shannon knew it was time for her to leave. More than anything, she wanted to give Janine a hug. But the signals had to come from the seven-year-old, and Janine didn't seem ready for that yet.

At the doorway Shannon said, ''Good night, Janine. You and Buster have pleasant dreams.''

Janine just waved at her, and Shannon went down the stairs and out the front door. There was an ache in her heart, and she had to figure out what was causing it.

Going over to the swing, she sat on it and studied the pattern of the stars in the sky. They were very bright tonight, and while she gazed up at them she realized the ache in her heart had more to do with her than with Janine. Yes, she wanted to help the little girl, but the bottom line was—she wanted a child of her own. She wanted the pleasure of tucking in her own son or daughter every night, of reading them countless stories, of hugging them whenever she could. Maybe she *did* need more in her life than the work she loved.

She didn't know how long she sat there, dreaming of a nursery and a baby and all the changes a child would make in her life. Absorbed in thinking about all of it, she was startled when the screen door opened and Rafe stepped outside.

Coming over to the swing, he sat beside her. "She doesn't seem to be afraid upstairs as long as she has Buster with her."

"He's her protector."

At that Rafe turned to look at her. "How do you do it?"

"What do you mean?"

"How do you talk to her and ask her questions and hold a conversation as if she's talking back to you?"

Shannon only hesitated a few moments. "She is."

"Do you want to explain that?" he asked gruffly.

"Since her mother died, you're waiting for her to speak, to utter those first words that will tell you everything's going to be all right again. You're completely focused on that. I'm not. She and I are developing a language that doesn't use words." She paused, then added, "There's body language, too. When she has her arms crossed, her head down, she's shutting everybody out. When she looks at me with her head tilted, her eyes directly on mine, she's curious or asking me a question."

"You've picked all of this up in two days?"

"This is what I do, Rafe. You put criminals behind bars. I read children. You could do it, too, if you're not thinking about what you're going to say next or what Janine might do next or the silence between you. You have to get past all that."

Maybe she could read Rafe's daughter, but she couldn't read him right now. He was looking at her with almost puzzlement in his eyes, as if he couldn't figure out who she was or what she did. Then she saw something else, and it almost took her breath away. It was admiration and...want? Did he want her?

The scent of roses drifted into the air that was as

silent as Shannon had ever known it. The silence only intensified the sensual humming between her and Rafe. Last night she'd backed away, telling herself it was the best thing to do...telling herself she had no choice.

She always had a choice. Last night, with the honesty of what had almost happened between them, she'd run because she was afraid. What would happen if she ever did really become captivated by a man? She never had been. She'd never wanted to be. Allen had been a try at something she'd known nothing about—a serious relationship and commitment. But she and Allen hadn't been right together, and she'd come away from that thinking she wouldn't be right for anyone.

Yet from the first moment she'd met Rafe's gaze...

She shivered, overcome by the magnitude of what *not* running away would mean.

Rafe reached over and brushed his hand gently up her arm. "Cold?"

She could say she was and scurry inside. That's probably why he'd asked. To give her a way out. To give them both a way out.

But she wasn't cold, and she shook her head, keeping her gaze on his.

His hand came to rest on her shoulder. "I've thought about kissing you sincc last night. It wouldn't be wise," he added, his voice deep with the desire she could feel emanating from him.

"No, it wouldn't be wise," she agreed in a whisper.

"You should go in."

"I wouldn't be able to sleep." She'd be wondering what a kiss of Rafe's would taste like. She'd be wishing she had stayed.

"Then maybe we should get this over with, so we both can get some sleep."

She knew what he meant, that anticipation was often better than reality. In this case, she guessed he would be wrong.

She was aware of the tightening tension in him, the press of his fingers on her shoulder signaling he was going to move closer. When he did, she leaned forward to meet him.

There was so much about Rafe she'd never noticed in other men. His brows were heavy, his hair thick with the hint of a wave. The lines in his forehead came from tension and worry, the crinkles around his eyes from forty years of living. As he slowly bent to her, it seemed she noticed a hundred different things, all of them enticing. All of them tempting. All of them exciting.

Maybe because of who he was, maybe because of what he did, she expected the kiss to be hard. Everything about Rafe was masterful. But when his lips covered hers, they were questing rather than demanding, searching rather than possessive. The movement and thrill and texture of him awakened desire she'd never known existed. Coherent thought fled as he opened his mouth over hers, and she entered dark, forbidden territory...forbidden because it could lead her someplace she had never been...maybe someplace she shouldn't go.

As Rafe's hot tongue swept her lower lip, *shouldn't* dissipated into the dark of night. The nature of the kiss changed, becoming hungry, becoming inciting. She slid her fingers into the hair at his temple, breathed in his scent, gave back the passion he was asking from her. Their tongues danced as a womanly ache she'd never known seemed to fill her whole being.

Abruptly Rafe tore away and swore.

Her pulse was racing so fast she didn't think it would ever slow again. The need Rafe had created inside of her more than matched anything he was feeling, and she couldn't understand the depth of it.

"*I* should have gone inside," he said tersely.

"You still can."

He looked over at her then, and in the moonlight his face was hard. "I will never get seriously involved in a relationship again."

"Rafe…"

"It's nonnegotiable, Shannon. I never want another woman to depend on me and look to me for protection. I never want to be married again and feel responsible for someone else's happiness."

"It was a kiss, Rafe," she said quietly.

"It sure as hell was. And you're a dreamer. I just wanted you to know where I stand."

Although her throat constricted, she managed, "Now I know."

With another salty epithet, he raked his hand through his hair and stood.

As he crossed to the door, she couldn't help but say, "Janine will heal, and you will, too."

"Concentrate on my daughter, Shannon, and forget about me."

Then he went inside, and the door clicked shut behind him.

Could she concentrate only on Janine? A soft little voice in Shannon's heart told her that would be impossible to do.

Chapter Four

At breakfast the next morning, Rafe denied the effects kissing Shannon had had on him. He told himself the softness of her voice as she spoke with his daughter, the way she pushed back curls that escaped her ponytail, the way her brown eyes skittered away from his, didn't affect him at all. He'd keep his distance, and what had happened last night wouldn't happen again.

But the tension between them was obvious enough for Cora to look at both of them curiously. The petite woman had the demeanor of a schoolmarm who knew and saw all.

As he finished up the last of his eggs and thought about breaking the awkward silence that had fallen over the table, Cora did it for him.

Standing, she went to the coffeepot and refilled all their cups. Then she said to Shannon, ''I forgot to tell you. The computer locked up again last night. I got so frustrated with it, I just shut the whole thing off. This morning when I turned all of it back on, the same thing happened again.''

Shannon dumped sugar into her coffee, lots of it. ''I guess I'll have to call Nolan again. Maybe he can send someone out.''

''That might not be necessary,'' Rafe suggested.

Shannon's gaze met his directly for the first time that morning. ''Why not?''

''I know my way around computers. Maybe I can have a look at it for you.''

Cora patted Rafe's shoulder as if he were a long-lost grandson. ''That would be wonderful. I really need to use it, and I don't want to wait for a repairman.'' Cora glanced at her niece. ''Maybe Rafe can figure out what's really wrong with it so it doesn't keep jamming.''

Shannon took a few sips of coffee. ''While you're doing that, Janine and I will spend some time with Marigold.''

Rafe knew exactly what Shannon was doing—taking advantage of the fact he'd be busy and would be out of her hair. He didn't like it. But she'd been right about one thing. He would have to trust her with Janine if therapy was going to work. Still, he wouldn't be too busy with the computer that he couldn't keep an eye on Janine, too.

''You're going to be in the front yard again?''

''No. We'll be in Marigold's corral.''

He remembered the shed and smaller corral adjoining the pasture behind the barn. If he was at the bunkhouse, he wouldn't be able to see a thing. Score one for the pretty therapist. He'd still check on them every now and then.

After Shannon and Janine went outside, Rafe asked Cora, "Is the office door open?"

"Sure is. The computer's in the reception area as soon as you walk in. Can't miss it."

Rafe went over to the window and watched Shannon and Janine, followed by Buster, as they crossed the lane.

"My niece is very good at what she does."

He glanced over his shoulder. "She's helped a lot of kids?"

"She sure has. She kept most of yesterday for Janine since it was her first day, but she has a full roster scheduled the rest of the week with her regular clients. I don't suppose she's told you she's even writing a book about it?"

Just in the short time he'd been around Shannon, he could see how multitalented she was, how she knew her strengths. Nancy had never known her strengths. Or maybe she'd always been afraid to find out what they were. Raised by affluent, older parents, she'd always been treated like a Dresden doll. She'd been so sweet, but so dependent...so needy, taking as much of everything as he could possibly give. Unlike Shannon, Nancy had been satisfied never to step out of the circle she'd drawn for herself where she felt safe and protected.

"Actually I think Shannon drives herself too hard," Cora went on. "But *slow down* isn't in that girl's vocabulary."

"Have you and Shannon always been close?"

Cora moved about the kitchen, storing leftover bacon, putting the milk in the refrigerator. "When Shannon and her mom moved to Sacramento, we all became closer than we'd ever been. Hannah, that's my sister, died when Shannon was in college, and Shannon moved in with me. Shannon bought this place, and she knew I was tired of working at my job as a claims adjuster for an insurance company. She asked if I wanted to come out here, run her office and help her. It's the best decision I've ever made.'' Cora winked at him. ''And if you can fix up my computer, all will be right in my world.''

He chuckled. ''I'll see what I can do.''

Fifteen minutes later he was in the office, figuring out what the problem was with the computer. Cora definitely needed more memory. That could be easily remedied. A more up-to-date program would help, too.

Rafe was about to shut down the computer until he could work with Cora on deleting files, when his elbow nudged a few papers alongside of the blotter on the desk. They fell to the floor. He guessed they'd been what Cora was working on when the computer had jammed. Stooping over, he picked them up. When he glanced at a letter written on a piece of paper torn from a notebook, an underlined word caught his eye. *Quackery.* He didn't hesitate to skim the letter.

Apparently the father of one of Shannon's patients had written to her, demanding his money back. He stated that his daughter's sessions with Shannon hadn't helped raise her grades, which was the reason he'd brought her to therapy to begin with. Horses might be fun, but they certainly weren't therapy, and Shannon wasn't going to pull the wool over his eyes or take his money.

Underneath the critical letter was one that Shannon had drafted for Cora to type. It asked Mr. Donneker to consider the changes in his daughter, Krissie, since she'd begun therapy. She also suggested he call and make an appointment so they could discuss the situation further.

Rafe had had his own doubts about equine therapy. Finding this letter from a disgruntled parent didn't quiet them.

Late that afternoon Rafe and Cora worked on the computer files while Janine played with kittens outside. After supper Rafe took Janine to the barn to visit the foal, fully expecting to see Shannon there. But she didn't appear, and he realized the stalls were already cleaned out. Cars had come and gone all day as Shannon had seen clients in her office and worked with them in the corral. He hadn't spotted her since supper.

An hour later, when he and Janine returned to the house, Cora was doing needlework. Janine went over to the sofa and sat beside her. Rafe couldn't help but wonder if Cora was sticking around because Shannon was absent.

Restless because he was used to working a full day and then some, he decided to find Shannon and ask her Janine's schedule for tomorrow. He could work on the fence while Janine was in session.

"Where did Shannon disappear to?" he asked Cora.

The older woman looked up and then frowned. "She's working on a project of hers."

"So I shouldn't disturb her?"

"Oh, I think it would be a good thing if you'd disturb her. She's out back, through the first stand of pines."

Janine appeared settled beside Cora, but he asked her, "Would you like to come with me?"

She looked at him then—really looked at him—and shook her head, pointing to what Cora was doing. She wanted to watch. Shannon had been right about Janine having her own language. He'd just been too worried about her to pick it up before. Today she hadn't seemed quite so distant. But maybe he was just looking for any little hint of progress, and it wasn't really there.

When Rafe rounded the porch and strode alongside the house, he passed cottonwoods and oaks, where an old wooden swing hung from the largest tree. He'd pushed Janine on it that afternoon. Veering away toward the pines, he couldn't hear noise of any kind, and he wondered what Shannon was doing back here. He walked on a path straight through the trees, a carpet of needles soft under his feet, and finally caught a flash of red. In a few steps he realized it was Shannon's T-shirt.

As he got closer, he saw she was using a shovel to dig out brush. Her jeans were soft and snug on her backside, and he could see the outline of her bra under her damp T-shirt. She'd pulled her hair up into a top-knot, and loose curls dangled here and there. Everything about her shouted WOMAN. He grew hard watching her, and he damned the response of his body he couldn't seem to control.

What in the hell was she doing?

She wasn't only adding brush to a pile under the trees, but there were stacks of stones, too. Was she trying to clear the land?

With all of her concentration on the stubborn brush, she didn't hear him approaching.

"I'm sure there's a very good reason you're doing hard labor."

At the sound of his voice she gave a small gasp, and the shovel fell from her hands.

"Sorry. Didn't mean to startle you," he said with a smile.

"You scared the daylights out of me! I hope Cora didn't send you out here to get me, because I'm not finished yet. I still have a good half hour of daylight."

"She didn't send me. I came looking for you on my own. She did say something about it not being a bad idea if I interrupted you. What *are* you doing?"

Shannon swiped her wrist across her brow and succeeded in leaving a streak of dirt along her forehead. "I want to put up a pavilion here. You know, one of those prefabricated ones? But I need to clear the land first."

"You can't be serious."

"Of course I'm serious. I want a place outside where I can bring the kids to draw or to sit and talk or to have a picnic."

"That I understand. Clearing the land is something altogether different."

She waved her arm across the area. "I have more than half of it finished."

"How long have you been working on it?"

"Since April."

He suddenly realized this was exactly what he needed—something physical...with a purpose. "I'll help you."

Her eyes widened. "I can't expect you to help. Besides, there's no need. I should be finished in another few weeks."

"Why wait a few weeks? I told you before, Shannon, I need something to do. And as far as a prefabricated pavilion goes, I can build you one myself, and it'll be a lot sturdier.'' When he saw she was about to protest, he added, "We can barter.''

As her tongue came out and licked her lips, he remembered everything about their kiss the night before. He forgot about bartering and thought only about kissing her again. This time, a lot more thoroughly.

"You've already paid me,'' she said.

"Only for the first two weeks. Since I've tasted Cora's cooking, I'd say you're not charging nearly enough for room and board.''

That brought a small smile to her lips. But she was still hesitant. "I don't know...''

"Think of this as *my* therapy, Shannon. You pay for the materials, I'll provide the labor. I can rent a saw if you don't have one.''

"I have a chain saw.''

"I need something with a little more finesse than that. Don't tell me you use the chain saw?''

"I haven't trained Buster to use it yet,'' she said dryly.

He laughed at that. "All right. I give up. You've shocked the hell out of all my preconceived notions of what a woman should do. But that doesn't mean you can't accept help. If put to the test, I can probably lift heavier rocks in a shorter amount of time.''

"Are we going to put it to the test?'' she returned, as if it was a dare.

"Not if you demur gracefully and accept my superior strength and knowledge in this matter.''

She shook her head and fought back another smile. "Do you have to work at being so arrogant?''

He grinned at her. "Actually, no. It comes naturally.''

They both laughed then, and Rafe realized he really

liked this woman, even though she could be frustrating and much too stubborn. He also realized he liked the challenge. One thing Nancy had never been was a challenge.

Unsettled by his comparison of the two women, he nodded to the wheelbarrow sitting by the mound of rocks. ''I'll work on the rocks if you want to keep digging out the brush.''

For the next twenty minutes or so, they worked silently, ever conscious of each other. Shannon had trouble keeping her gaze away from the expanse of Rafe's broad shoulders, his strong arms, even his hands, as he lifted stones and rocks and placed them in the wheelbarrow. Everything about him was exceedingly male. For that reason she was protecting herself with a little more independence than usual. Their kiss had told her that Rafe's passion could shatter the wall she'd put up around herself, could make her feel and need and want in ways that terrified her.

How had her mother felt about her father when they'd first met? How long had it been until she realized he was abusive? Shannon had never had those questions answered, and she never would. She'd thought she'd accepted that. She'd thought she'd put all of it in the past. But Rafe stirred up every emotion and every fear she'd thought she'd analyzed. His desires seemed to be a direct line to both heaven and hell, and she didn't want to make a decision that would put her on the road to either. She liked it where she was. She liked being safe. It was all she'd ever dreamed of as a child.

Darkness fell like a slow curtain descending, and Shannon dug more brush, using the time as best she could, trying not to be so completely aware of Rafe, remembering the elderly couple who'd lived next door to her and her mom after they'd gotten their own apartment in Sacramento. Bud and Ellie had been in their seventies, married for fifty years. Shannon had visited them often. They'd teased each other, argued once in a while and depended on each other. They'd given her a vision of the relationship a man and woman *could* have if they were committed, if they held on, if they were kind to each other.

With her mind not completely on what she was doing, Shannon's hands slipped on the shovel and she scraped a blister. She made a soft sound that carried in the dusk.

Coming over to her, Rafe asked, "What happened?"

Embarrassed she'd caught his attention, she just shook her head. "It's my own fault. I should be wearing gloves."

"Let me see."

Before she could protest, before she could prepare herself, he took her hand and turned it palm up. As he examined it, his thumb slid along the line of her fingers, and a trembling began deep inside of her.

She should have drawn her hand away. She *would* have drawn her hand away. But his skin on hers was so hot, so gentle, so absolutely mesmerizing, that she could only stand there hoping he'd touch her longer.

Her heart was racing so fast she could barely breathe.

Rafe began to lower his head, began to raise her hand to his lips. She held her breath.

Then suddenly the moment was broken. His jaw tensed as his head came up and his fingers slid away from her hand, setting it free. "It's getting too dark to work. We should go in."

Too dark...too hot...too intimate. The fall of deep night could release too many emotions they were holding in check, emotions that could bring them together in a way daylight wouldn't.

She backed away from Rafe, walked over to the wheelbarrow and laid the shovel across the top of it. Rafe Pierson unglued her, and she'd better figure out how to hold herself together.

On Saturday morning Rafe went into the barn and headed for the back where tools were stored. He wanted to take an inventory to see if there was anything else he might need to start the pavilion after the land was cleared. He'd spent his free time the past two days repairing fence. He didn't know how Shannon did it, but practically singlehandedly she kept the place in fairly good shape. On his past visits to the tool section of the barn, he'd found what he'd needed and that was that. But today he noticed a blanket covering something and he decided to investigate.

Suddenly the barn door opened and Clancy came in carrying a pitchfork. The teenager had been dropped off yesterday around noon and worked till five. Rafe hadn't seen much of him then. This morning he'd arrived around eight.

"Clancy," he said in acknowledgment.

The boy looked over, saw Rafe and frowned. "Are you going to be doing something in here?" the teenager asked, a bit defiantly.

"Not for long. I'm starting work on a pavilion for Shannon at the end of the week, and wanted to see what I might need."

Clancy's dark eyes grew rounder. "You are?"

"Yeah. Why so surprised?"

"No reason," the boy mumbled. He started walking toward the horses' stalls, but then turned back. "I heard you were a district attorney or something."

"My official title is deputy district attorney."

"And that means you're one of the guys who puts people in jail."

There was a wariness in Clancy's eyes, and Rafe wondered what it was all about. "I put criminals in jail if there's evidence against them."

Clancy's face seemed to flush a bit, but Rafe couldn't tell for sure. The boy said, "Well, I gotta get to the stalls."

Rafe watched the teenager stride away, thinking about how he reminded Rafe of himself at that age. Sullen defiance had been a coat of armor.

The blanket on the shelf drew Rafe again and he pulled it aside, looking at the contraption underneath. He smiled. It was an ice cream maker! Shannon had probably put the blanket over it to keep the dust off. The direction booklet was even tucked beside the mixing paddle, and he paged through it.

Maybe Janine would like to make ice cream. Even though it was Saturday, Rafe knew Shannon was seeing clients all day. It would be a nice treat for her, too. He and Janine could go into town and pick up everything they needed. It would give them a way to fill the afternoon. Back in Salinas his daughter had shied away from crowds, but the supermarket in Fawn Grove should be less bustling. Still, remembering what Shannon had said about giving his daughter power, if she didn't want to go, he'd make the trip himself.

* * *

Fawn Grove was a farm town. As Rafe drove down the main street later that afternoon with Janine beside him, he passed a park with a baseball field, a library that looked as old as the town and a community center that appeared fairly new. After he crossed the railroad tracks, he saw a storefront proclaiming Constantine's Computers, and he made a sudden decision.

Slowing, he parked along the street at a parking meter. "I'd like to pick up something for Shannon's computer. Is it all right if we stop here first?" he asked his daughter. As an incentive he added, "We might even find a game to play on the laptop I brought along." The computer sat on the dresser in his room, but he hadn't started it up yet.

Janine thought about it and gave him an interested nod.

He smiled, thinking that maybe they *were* making progress, and opened his door.

Once inside, Rafe showed Janine to the section where the games were shelved. In the same aisle he found the software programs, and he picked up one he thought Cora could use easily. They'd solved the memory problem for the time being by deleting some of the older files, but he also picked up everything he would need to install more memory.

There hadn't been anyone at the cashier's desk when they'd walked in, but a bell had rung. Now Nolan Constantine himself came down an aisle from the back of the store. When he saw Rafe he stopped. "Mr. Pierson, isn't it?" There was no warmth in Constantine's fake smile.

"Yes. And you're the Constantine in Constantine's Computers?"

"Sure am. It's all mine. Two stores and a third opening soon. I'm only on counter duty today because my manager's sick. Did Shannon send you for something special?"

"Shannon didn't send me at all. Actually, Cora's been having some trouble with the computer so I thought I'd spend some time updating it."

At that Constantine frowned. "Shannon knows I'll take care of that for her anytime she wants."

When the man spoke of Shannon, there was a proprietary air that Rafe didn't like. In fact, he didn't like Nolan Constantine at all. In his work Rafe wore suits and ties because they were part of his profession. But he was much more comfortable in sweats or jeans. Constantine, on the other hand, in his custom-made suit, white shirt and silk tie looked as if every day was an occasion to look his best. He was too full of his own importance, Rafe decided.

Feeling territorial, knowing he had no right to, Rafe added, "I had to come into town for some supplies for the pavilion I'm putting up for Shannon."

"A pavilion?"

If Constantine didn't know about it, he decided Shannon must not confide in the man very much. But who knew? Maybe they had other things to talk about...or do.

Janine came up beside her dad then and handed him a package. It was a game that helped in learning math, and he smiled at her. "That's a good choice."

Constantine just frowned as he rang up Rafe's purchases. After he bagged them, he handed the package to Rafe. "Tell Shannon I'll see her after church tomorrow."

Church. He hadn't been in a church much over the years—Janine's christening...Nancy's funeral. He suddenly wondered if Nolan Constantine went to church to mingle with the parishioners, or because he actually had faith in something outside of himself. Any faith Rafe had once nurtured had been destroyed the day Nancy died and Janine stopped talking.

Rafe didn't respond to Constantine, just picked up his purchase, took Janine's hand and bade the store owner a polite goodbye.

When Rafe and Janine returned to the Rocky R later that afternoon, they showed Cora the supplies they'd bought to make ice cream. She'd decided to put them in the refrigerator in her digs so they could surprise Shannon. Then while Janine went with Cora to "help" with supper, Rafe worked on Shannon's computer. He installed the additional memory and was working with the software when Shannon came into the office's reception area, carrying a file folder. She looked tired.

"Finished for the day?" he asked.

"No. I have one more appointment. Patty should be arriving any minute. Did Cora have a problem with the computer again?"

"Nope. And she won't have any more problems, not once she transfers the billing to this new software."

Shannon came over to the desk, looking puzzled. "What new software?"

"I went into town to rent a radial-arm saw so I can start on the pavilion by the end of the week. When I saw the computer shop, I decided to remedy your problems for you."

Shannon's eyes became a darker brown as she said evenly, "I didn't ask you to remedy my problems."

He could tell from her tone she was upset, and he

didn't understand why. "It'll be a lot easier for Cora if the computer isn't constantly jamming."

"How much did all of this cost?" The edge in her voice should have warned him.

Motioning to the desk chair, he responded, "The receipt's in the bag. But you don't have to worry about paying me back."

"Of course I have to worry about paying you back!" she exploded. "It's a business expense. This is *my* business, not yours. Why did you do this without asking me first?"

He'd simply been trying to do her a favor, and now he was getting annoyed, too. "I thought you'd appreciate someone who knew what he was doing—"

She cut in without letting him finish. "What I don't appreciate is a man foisting his solution on me."

"Hey, look. If you don't want to use the software, then don't. But I think Cora's going to be grateful, even if you aren't."

A car's tires sounded on the gravel outside, and Shannon swung around to peer out the window.

The manila folder still in her hand, she came around to the back of the desk where he was standing. "Excuse me, I have to get into the file cabinet."

She might have been working with the horses all day, but she still smelled like a woman, and the scent of her gripped Rafe as it always did. Instead of moving out in front of the desk, he stepped beside the file cabinet. Maybe it was sheer perversity, but he couldn't help tempting them both.

When she looked up at him, her brown eyes flashed, but she didn't say a word. She just pulled open the drawer, arranged the file inside and slammed it shut.

Before she could take the offensive again, he

pointed to the computer tower. "You have enough memory now to run anything you want. I could dismantle it, but your computer will just lock up again. I don't imagine you want that."

Standing her ground only a few inches from him, Shannon met his gaze squarely. "I don't like someone taking over my life, Rafe."

"What you don't like," he snapped, "is someone giving you help when you need it."

"What I don't like is a man telling me what I need!" The words reverberated in the small room.

Turning away from him and the attraction between them, she didn't give him a backward glance as she sailed out the door.

Chapter Five

By Saturday evening Shannon realized that she'd overreacted with Rafe. It had been a particularly long day, and she'd been hot and tired. She hated to turn clients away, and she was getting more and more referrals. Still, that didn't explain how upset she'd been with Rafe.

Somehow they'd gotten through supper with puzzled looks from Cora and even Janine. Shannon just needed to be away from Rafe now, and as she worked with the filly in the barn, she thought about why.

That morning in her session with Janine, she'd taught the little girl how to lead Marigold, how to be somewhat assertive with the pony. Janine had had a hard time understanding that if Marigold wanted to stop to eat grass, she didn't have to let her. It was a lesson to show Janine she had some control over those around her.

Shannon wished *she* had learned that lesson much younger.

This afternoon Rafe had said he was simply trying to do her a favor. But it had felt as if he was trying to take control of her and her office. Maybe with another man she could have accepted it, but with Rafe…

It was so disturbing to her that she could still feel and taste his kiss. She didn't want a man to have that power to unsettle her. She didn't want a man to have power over her at all. She could remember all too well her mother's marriage and the power her father had always exerted.

Throughout supper her heart had been having a tug-of-war with her head. She knew she should apologize to Rafe, and yet if she did, she was afraid she'd get closer to him. He was so different from Allen. So different from Nolan. So different from any man she'd ever met.

Darkness had fallen by the time she left the barn, and she could see the light from inside the house glowing onto the porch. It looked as if Cora, Rafe and Janine were all outside. As she approached she realized Rafe was crouched down beside something… And then she saw what it was—the ice cream maker.

Stepping up onto the porch, she asked, "What's going on?"

"Rafe and Janine decided to make ice cream for all of us," Cora said. "I just cut up a few strawberries to put on top. Are you going to have some with us?"

"I didn't know we had the ingredients to make ice cream."

"Oh, Janine and Rafe got them when they went into town today."

Janine was happily slurping ice cream as she sat on the swing next to Cora.

"Is it good?" Shannon asked the little girl.

Janine bobbed her head enthusiastically and gave Shannon a smile. She smiled more now, and that pleased Shannon.

But when Shannon turned to look at Rafe, she saw that he was unsmiling, and she knew she had to talk to him...alone. First, though, she had to get through a few scoops of ice cream.

Rafe spooned the rich vanilla into a dish for her and she took it. "Thank you. Whose idea was this?"

"I found the machine in the barn this morning."

"I'd forgotten we had it." Moving to a lawn chair, she sat and sampled the dessert. "It's delicious. Have you made ice cream before?"

"Once, a very long time ago. I just followed the instructions. There's really nothing to it if you can read."

That wasn't entirely true. The rock salt had to be added consistently to the ice to keep the contents of the canister at the right temperature. The electric machine did most of the work, but there was still a trick to it. Homemade ice cream could sometimes turn out like soup.

Suddenly Janine hopped off the swing, brought her dish to Rafe and pointed inside.

"You can watch the movie now if you'd like," he told her. "Do you need me to put it in?"

She shook her head and handed him the dish. Then she opened the door, let Buster precede her and went in. A few moments later they heard the sound of the TV and then a Walt Disney movie beginning.

Shannon guessed they'd bought the movie in town today, too.

Cora stood and asked Shannon, "Would you like more?"

"No. This is fine."

"Then I'm going to take the rest of it inside, pack up what's left and clean up the machine."

"I'll carry it in for you," Rafe said as he stood.

Shannon's heart beat faster as Rafe took the canister from the ice cream maker inside. She could hear the movie playing on the TV, the low rumble of Rafe's and Cora's voices. Her heart raced faster as she wondered if Rafe would come back out—and what she would say if he did.

After she finished the dessert, she felt restless. Setting her dish beside her chair, she stood and went to sit on the step, gazing at the light at the top of the barn, then at the moon above.

Since she'd been a child, she'd been attuned to every sound of the night. That vigilance came from being afraid her father's temper would erupt after he'd had a few glasses of bourbon before bed—afraid he'd slam open the door of her room and come after her, as he often went after her mother. There had been a few times, when he'd come in and stood by her bed shouting at her, that she'd feared it was her turn to feel the back of his hand.

Why were these thoughts returning now? She'd turned the page on all of it and written lots of new ones. Good ones. Hopeful ones.

At the sound of Rafe's boots, her stomach fluttered. He'd started wearing them the day he'd repaired the fence. He stopped in the living room for a few moments and commented on the movie, and then he came outside.

Propped against the rail, she turned to look up at him. "The ice cream was a great idea. Janine seemed to enjoy it."

"You should have seen her licking the paddles and Buster licking her face." His voice was husky, as if just the thought of it touched him deeply.

Rafe Pierson was such a fascinating man. She had no doubt that he could be ruthless with criminals. Yet he could also be so very tender with his daughter.

In the sky above, Shannon could hear the hum of a jet, and it seemed incongruous with the sound of cicadas, with the scent of roses and earth, with her feelings toward Rafe causing her turmoil.

He came over and sat on the step beside her. She knew she owed him an apology. "I'm sorry," she murmured. "I overreacted this afternoon."

His jean-clad knee lightly grazed hers. "Why did you?"

It was too complicated to explain, and she didn't even know if she wanted to. "It doesn't matter."

He was quiet for a few moments. "You don't talk much about yourself, do you?"

"No."

"Maybe you were trained too well in listening."

"Maybe." Although she hadn't told him much, Rafe was beginning to know her.

After the silence stretched between them for a few moments he asked, "Have you ever been married?" There was curiosity in his voice, maybe more.

"No. I was engaged once, though."

"How long ago?" he asked.

"About two years, now."

"What happened?"

She could refuse to answer. She could tell him she didn't like being given the third degree, which must come as second nature to him. But this time, with this man, she felt the need to confide just a little. "He said I devoted too much time and attention to the Rocky R. I bought it two months after I'd agreed to marry him."

"*Did* you give it too much time and attention?"

"No. Not if I wanted to get it up and running. On the other hand, I think buying it was my way of pulling away from Allen."

After Rafe thought about that, he asked, "Why did you agree to marry him?"

She'd analyzed the reasons over and over since then. "I wanted the family I'd never had. I wanted children. I wanted—" She shook her head. "I wanted happily-ever-after." In the hush of night with Rafe beside her, the idea of happily-ever-after unnerved her.

"Did *you* call it off?"

She shook her head. "No. He did. He said he wouldn't compete with my career. Or with horses and chores. Or with kids that weren't even my own."

"Why did you get engaged to the guy?" There was a roughness in Rafe's voice that said she should have been a better judge of character.

But Rafe didn't know her fiancé had been everything her father hadn't been. "Allen was an accountant. He had a secure job, looked good in a tie and was a great dancer."

"That's it?"

"That's all I'm going to tell you," she murmured.

Allen had been well mannered, well educated, well practiced in being charming. He'd swept her off her feet. But by the time he started making the decisions for both of them, when he'd decided where and when they were going to get married and how many people would be at their wedding, when he'd complained about her time at the Rocky R and called off the wedding, she'd known marriage to him never would have worked out.

"Your parents' divorce set you up to want more than they had," Rafe decided.

It had been much more than her parents' divorce. It had been Bud and Ellie. It had been the wish to believe she could find a soul mate. "What about *your* parents? What kind of marriage did they have?"

Silent for a few moments, he finally answered, "My parents weren't married. My father left before I was born. And my mother... Men came and went until she was in an accident when I was eight. She was on a motorcycle with one of her boyfriends without a helmet."

He said it so matter-of-factly, and yet she knew it wasn't. There was so much he wasn't saying. "Who raised you?"

"An assortment of foster parents, none of whom I liked very much. Most of them didn't give a fig about me, just the money I brought in."

"Rafe..."

"Don't go all compassionate on me, Shannon. I survived. I grew up tough and smart. I took advantage of scholarships to college, and I never looked back."

Understanding the need not to look back all too well, she didn't probe further. Sitting here beside Rafe, discussing his background and her ex-fiancé, seemed too intimate. "I guess we'd better go in," she said softly. "I want to get a long shower and then do some reading I've put aside too many nights now."

Rafe shifted on the step, and his arm brushed hers. Her gaze gravitating to his, she wished she hadn't mentioned the shower. Something about the thought of it, him thinking about it, too—

Under the light spilling out from the living room she could see that he *was* thinking about it. There were sparks of desire in his eyes.

"Your perfume's nice." He leaned just a bit closer.

"It's not perfume. It's soap."

His voice was low as he added, "You smell like flowers."

"Honeysuckle," she murmured.

"It suits you."

She was an idiot to sit here like this, remembering everything he'd said after he'd kissed her—how he never wanted to be involved in another serious relationship. Yet she was mightily attracted to him. Not just physically, but emotionally, too. She couldn't help wishing so many things were different. That he wasn't still tied up in turmoil about his wife and daughter. That she herself could be more trusting with her feelings, confident a man could want her for who she was, not afraid one would take over her life.

"What are you thinking?" he asked, his breath warm, his mouth so very close to hers.

"About what you said the other night. We shouldn't be…be…" The thought fled as she inhaled his scent. Pulling herself together, she went on, "Maybe we should just concentrate on becoming…friends."

Raising his head then, he almost growled, "You seem to think men and women can *be* friends. I don't see how when there's more on their minds than talking.''

There was more on *her* mind than talking. She couldn't deny it.

He pushed himself to his feet. ''You go take your shower, Shannon. I'll put Janine to bed. I'm sure we'll both dream of vanilla ice cream and horses when we shut our eyes tonight.''

As Rafe went inside, she realized he was telling her that she was deluding herself if she thought they could be simply friends. Was she?

At breakfast the following morning, Cora invited Rafe and Janine to go along to church with them. To Shannon's surprise he accepted the offer. Telling herself preparations had nothing to do with Rafe, she took particular care with dressing, reminding herself she always did when she went to church. It was her one chance during the week to get out of her jeans.

But this morning her pink-and-turquoise silky blouse and matching slim skirt, made her feel particularly feminine. She'd done something different with her hair, too.

When she came into the living room, Rafe and Janine were descending the steps.

''Don't you look pretty!'' she said to Janine, who was wearing a mint-green pinafore dress and patent-leather shoes. When Shannon looked up at Rafe, his broad shoulders in a suitcoat and the impressive length of him in the charcoal slacks made her mouth go dry.

Janine was pointing to Shannon's hair and smiling.

She turned her attention from father to daughter. ''You like it? Would you like me to do your hair like this? We have a few minutes.''

The French-braiding was second nature to Shannon. She used to do it a lot more often to keep her curls tamed.

Shannon went to her room for a brush, elastic bands and ribbons, then sat on the sofa while Janine knelt on the floor. By the time Cora came to the door, Shannon had completed two braids and had even tied bows on them.

Shannon took Janine to her bedroom to show her how her hair looked, using a hand mirror along with the dresser mirror. After Janine had studied it for a few moments, she threw her arms around Shannon, giving her a huge hug.

Shannon felt a rush of affection and something that went even deeper than that. Overjoyed, she returned the hug, knowing this was a big step for the little girl, hoping words might soon follow.

As she straightened she saw Rafe in the doorway. He was watching them with an odd expression. He cleared his throat. ''Cora said to tell you she forgot her sweater and she'll meet us at my car.''

''You're driving?''

''Cora mentioned her car doesn't always start. And I thought we'd be more comfortable in mine than in a pickup. Unless you want to take two vehicles.''

His car would definitely be more comfortable than her truck. ''We're finished here. I think Janine likes her new hairdo. I might have to teach you how to do it.''

His smile was wry. ''If you can teach me that, you can teach me anything.''

Her heart gave a hopeful little skip, and she wondered if that was true. Could she teach him to move on with his life? If she could, she guessed he had quite a few things he could teach her, too.

The church Shannon attended was white clapboard, pristine against its setting of oaks and pines. Oleander grew out front on either side of the steps. The church's steeple reached high to the sky, and the bell there rung resoundingly, announcing service time.

After Rafe parked in the gravel lot, he opened the back door on his side for Cora, then came around and opened the doors for Shannon and Janine. Janine stayed close by Shannon's side as they crossed to the church steps. Then she tucked her hand into Shannon's.

The simple gesture touched Shannon as she leaned close to the little girl. "You let me know if you get tired of listening or sitting, and we'll come outside for a few minutes. Okay?"

Janine nodded, and Shannon knew Rafe had caught what she'd said.

On the way up the steps he murmured close to her ear, "It looks as if she's becoming attached to you." She couldn't tell if he was pleased about it, disgruntled or simply making an observation.

The minister was a short, jovial man with thinning gray hair and small, oval, wire-rimmed glasses. During his sermon, his wit brought smiles, as well as a few bursts of laughter from his congregation. Shannon noticed Rafe listening intently, though he didn't smile and laugh with the others or sing the age-old songs that always roused faith and emotion in Shannon. Had he come today searching for answers? Had he come for his daughter's sake? Was going to church a ritual that brought sanity when the rest of life was disordered?

After the service, while they were standing in the vestibule waiting to greet the minister before they exited, Nolan Constantine came up to Shannon and dropped his arm around her shoulders. "You look very pretty this morning."

"Hi, Nolan. You remember Mr. Pierson and his daughter, Janine?"

"Mr. Pierson and I talked when he came into the store. I told him to tell you I'd see you here today."

When Shannon glanced at Rafe, he didn't look guilty at all that he hadn't passed on the message.

"It must have slipped my mind," he told Nolan.

Shannon could see her aunt's lips twitching as Cora turned away to talk to the minister and casually clasped Janine's shoulder as she did. The little girl went with her.

Nolan said to Shannon, "No matter. I just wanted to remind you, I still have tickets to that concert this evening. Why don't you come along with me and take a break from the Rocky R?"

Nolan knew how hard she worked. When he'd asked her to the concert last week, she'd told him she didn't know how busy her schedule might be, with Rafe and his daughter arriving.

When she looked at Rafe, she remembered their conversation last night, her desire to be friends, his doubt that that's all they'd be. Living in the same house with him increased the intimacy she felt growing between them. She needed a break from that more than from the Rocky R.

Ignoring the magnetic pull toward Rafe, she made a quick decision and smiled at Nolan. "Going to the concert sounds like a good idea. What time should I be ready?"

* * *

"Say you'll accept the money, Shannon," Nolan prompted after they returned from their evening out and parked in front of the ranch house. "There are no strings except for the news conference."

It would probably take Shannon the next few years and then some to come up with the money for the indoor riding ring. "I suppose you'd want a plaque on the outside of the building?"

"That would be a nice gesture," Nolan said with a grin.

Shannon laughed. He was an out-and-out publicity hound and didn't hide the fact. There was a certain charm in that. They'd had a nice evening. Nolan was a good conversationalist and always excellent company. She just didn't *feel* anything for him except the ease of being with a friend. And if this was friendship, what bubbled between her and Rafe was definitely a lot more.

"All right, Nolan. You get a tax write-off and as much publicity as you can generate, and I'll get an indoor ring. You'll have a lifetime invitation to come riding whenever you like."

He laughed. "Then you know I won't be around much because I've told you how I feel about horses, *and* what goes with them."

She laughed then asked, "Would you like to come in for a cup of coffee?" She noticed the living room light was still on and guessed Rafe was probably watching TV. "Rafe might still be up, but we could talk in the kitchen."

"I don't think I'll come in tonight. I'll call you and we can set up a time one evening next week. Maybe you can come into town and we'll have dinner."

"All right." When she opened the door and would have slid out of the car, he caught her arm. "You and Pierson. It's not a problem having him in your house, is it?"

The genial atmosphere between them slid away. "I'm not sure what you mean."

Nolan looked chagrined in the glow of the overhead light. "It's pretty cozy, you two being there all hours together. Maybe Cora should be sleeping in the house while he's there."

"I'm not sure why you're concerned, Nolan."

He shrugged. "Appearances and all."

"I've never put much store in appearances. This is only temporary."

"How temporary?"

"He's taken a leave of absence until August." She paused, then began, "Nolan, if this money has any strings at all..."

He released her arm and put up his hands in a stop motion. "No strings. I told you that. I'm just concerned about your reputation."

"My reputation will be fine. Trust me. I'll see you next week." Then she slid out of his car, wondering if she was making a mistake accepting his donation.

As she waved and Nolan drove away she was still wondering.

Shannon was worrying about her decision when she opened the screen door and stepped inside the house. It was almost midnight, and the news channel flickered on the TV set. Rafe was stretched out on the couch in gray sweats and a white T-shirt, his feet bare. He looked at home, rumpled and so very sexy.

His gaze flicked to her, and he switched off the TV with the remote, sitting up slowly. "Did you have a good time?" he asked. There was more than casual interest in his voice.

She laid her purse on the pine table by the stairs. "It was pleasant."

When Rafe stood, his green eyes were intense. "Was the time you spent outside in the car with Constantine pleasant, too?"

"We were talking."

"That sounds like a teenage excuse. You had all night to talk."

She thought about reminding him that it was none of his business, but instead she just responded, "I'm too old to make out in a car, if that's what you're insinuating."

His voice deepened as he came closer to her. "If the stars are lined up right, you're never too old to make out in a car."

Just the thought of sitting in a car with Rafe, kissing him, touching him… She had to get her mind off that track and fast.

"Nolan and I were discussing the offer he made to donate money for an indoor ring." She didn't even know why she was explaining, but the way Rafe was looking at her she felt she had to.

"That would be a bad idea."

"There would be no strings, Rafe. Nolan insisted on that. He wants the publicity, and maybe a plaque on the building. I believe him when he says this is just an altruistic venture because he believes in my work."

"Stop wearing blinders, Shannon. I've known very few true philanthropists. Nolan Constantine doesn't even come close."

"You don't know him."

"Don't forget what I do for a living, what I see and

what I deal with every day. It all involves judging human nature.''

''So does what *I* do,'' she protested.

''Maybe so. But in this case Constantine has the means to give you something you want. That could be clouding your judgment about him. Or is something else clouding your judgment about him?''

Beard stubble lined Rafe's jaw. It was as black as his hair. In that instant she knew her judgment about Nolan wasn't clouded at all. Everything she was feeling about Rafe was another matter entirely. She felt turned upside down whenever she was around him. Now was certainly no exception. Dressed as he was, looking as he did, he exuded raw male power that excited her in a way that was fascinating.

''Nothing about Nolan is clouding my judgment,'' she insisted.

Rafe reached out and clasped her shoulders then, gently but firmly. The current that was always zipping around them found a closed circuit, seemed to pass through her body and then back to him. She saw the aliveness of it in his eyes. She felt the sparks of it through her fingertips.

''Are you interested in Nolan Constantine just as a philanthropist or as a man, too?'' he demanded gruffly.

Her gaze went to Rafe's lips, and she remembered exactly how they'd felt on hers. ''Why does it matter?''

''Because I want to kiss you again. I won't if you belong to another man.''

''I'll never belong to *any* man,'' she flung back defiantly.

There was a flicker of surprise in Rafe's gaze, but

then he pushed harder. ''Do you have something going on with Nolan Constantine?''

''No. We're just friends.'' She knew, when she said it, what would happen next, and she tried to prepare herself. But when Rafe's arms went around her and his head bent to hers, she wasn't prepared at all.

Before his lips touched hers, he growled, ''When the black of night hits, all I can think about is kissing you.'' Then he was.

Her world was already rocking when his tongue advanced and conquered her lips, easing them apart, pushing inside. Her trembling had already begun when his arms wrapped around her, and now it shook her, along with the sensuality of everything about Rafe Pierson.

The hot invasion of his tongue made her breath hitch, and a tide of sensation washed over her, attempting to drown her. She couldn't think, she could only feel. That was so foreign to her...so exceptionally wonderful. With her arms twined around his neck, she could feel the tension in his shoulders, and she wondered if he was trembling inside, too. She clung to him as he angled the kiss and took it deeper, growling low in his throat, shuddering as she responded and stroked him back. They were headed into the swirl of a hurricane, and Shannon didn't know if anything would ever be the same again.

Rafe's large hands molded her to him as he caressed her back ever downward until he reached her bottom. He pulled her up into him, and she gasped from the sheer pleasure of it. She slid her hands into his hair, wanting to feel so much more of him, wanting to get closer, wanting so many things she couldn't even name.

Breaking away from her suddenly, he let out a harsh groan and murmured, "Damn, we'd be good together." Then he was kissing her again...rocking against her...making her need, too.

His words kept sounding in her head. *We'd be good together.* But a small voice of reason that managed to make its way in asked, *Good for what? He already said he's not interested in a relationship.*

Shannon realized she was in way over her head. She'd never known a man who could make her feel and want like this. The shock of it had dazzled her...hypnotized her...made her forget who she was and who he was.

Using all of the strength within her to remember, she raised her hands against his shoulders and pushed away from him.

He looked down on her, his eyes glazed with the passion she was still feeling. "What's wrong?" His voice was raspy, and she didn't even know if she could find hers.

"*This* is wrong. We can't do this. I can't do this."

"We *were* doing this."

If she was hot before, she felt her cheeks flare even redder, now. "I don't want a fling that'll leave us both broken when you leave."

"Broken? Hell, we'd be satisfied. You're old enough to know what pleasure is. We could take our fill of it."

All too clearly she knew she didn't want just pleasure from Rafe, and that scared her even more than his sensuality did, more than the ravages of an affair did. "I'm not like that," she murmured, not knowing what else to say, unable to tell him her feelings for him were growing much too fast and much too strong.

"Now let me get this straight. You'll accept a ton of money from Constantine, but from me you don't want to accept a computer program—or a night that might make us forget everything about the day."

"Nolan's just...a friend," she reminded him again lamely.

He raked his hand through his hair and then strode over to the stairway. "Yeah. I got that. So I guess I'm still a stranger. After a kiss like that, I have to wonder if you haven't kissed a lot more strangers than friends." After firing that shot, he mounted the stairs and disappeared to the second floor.

It had been a very long time since Shannon had cried. Really cried. As tears burned in her eyes now, she blinked them away.

Chapter Six

While Shannon was cleaning out a stall the next morning, she suddenly realized Janine was no longer playing with the kittens close by. After breakfast Rafe's daughter had tugged on Shannon's hand and pointed toward the barn, indicating she wanted to go along with her. Rafe had said that was fine with him, since he'd be clearing the land in the backyard. That was about *all* he'd said to her this morning.

The atmosphere was definitely tense between them, and they were going to have to do something about that. But Rafe hadn't seemed in the mood this morning to mend fences. Truth be told, she hadn't been ready to try, either. She'd relived their kiss and their bodies molding together over and over throughout the night, and she'd actually looked forward to mucking out the stalls this morning—because she knew her feet would be firmly planted in reality there.

Suspecting where Janine had disappeared to, Shannon went outside and stood under the overhang, catching a glimpse of her by Marigold's corral.

Janine had pulled grass from the ground and was holding it out to Marigold to eat. The pony nuzzled Janine's hand, taking the grass easily. Then Janine did something that made Shannon's heart thud more rapidly. She got very close to the fence and the pony. The pony nuzzled the seven-year-old's neck, and Janine made a sound. Shannon watched and listened carefully as Janine stepped away and then moved closer again. Marigold greeted her like an old friend, nuzzling her hair under her ear until Janine actually giggled!

Shannon could clearly hear the happy sound coming from Janine, and she wanted to rush to her, throw her arms around her and hug her. Yet she knew she couldn't. If Janine caught her watching, she might go back into her shell, and Shannon didn't want that to happen. Quietly she returned to the barn, laid fresh straw in the stall and then checked on Janine again. The little girl was petting Marigold, leaning very close to her, and Shannon wondered if she was whispering. Wouldn't that be a miracle! Talking to the pony didn't mean she was ready to talk to the adults around her, but it was certainly a start.

Throughout the morning as Shannon saw other clients, she debated with herself about telling Rafe what she'd seen. She had to separate what had happened last night with him from her relationship with Janine and what was happening with the little girl. That was very difficult to do.

That evening after supper Rafe found Shannon in the barn in the stall with the new foal. She was running her hands over her and talking to her softly.

"Where's the mare?" he asked.

"Outside. Got to get this little lady used to me so I can eventually introduce her to a halter."

In the silence that ensued, Shannon knew they were both probably thinking of their parting the night before.

Before she could figure out what to say, Rafe told her his reason for coming to the barn. "I thought I'd take one of the horses for a ride. Cora and Janine are playing pitch and fetch with Buster, so it seemed like a good time."

"Want some company?" Shannon asked casually.

"You're not too busy?"

"I'm never too busy to go on a trail ride. Besides, since you've been helping out with some of the chores, I'm caught up." Rafe had cleaned out the stalls she hadn't had time to do first thing in the morning.

"I wouldn't mind the company," he said casually. "I'm sure you know some great trails it would take me a while to find. I'd like to do more than ride the fence line."

"I can show you a couple of different trails. Then if you want to go exploring, you can."

Less than fifteen minutes later Shannon had saddled her horse, Gray Lady, and Rafe had saddled and mounted a chestnut mare named Rock-A-Bye. As they rode along the fence line a ways, Shannon could see that Rafe was a natural rider and could easily handle himself on a horse. She suspected he could handle himself anywhere.

Eventually they turned away from the fence and trotted along the fields, turning yellow in the mid-June heat. Rows of corn rose toward the sun as the breeze swept by them, and the horses ran on the packed dirt. They slowed their mounts as they neared a peach orchard directly up ahead.

"Is this yours?" Rafe asked as Shannon rode up beside him.

"No. It belongs to my neighbor. Fortunately for me, the Rocky R was on a small parcel of land. I couldn't have afforded it otherwise."

"Are your neighbors friendly?" he asked with a wry grin.

"They won't shoot on sight," she said with a smile, and then immediately realized what she'd said. She saw his expression turn grim. "I'm sorry, Rafe. That was thoughtless."

"No, it wasn't. It's an idiom from a time when guns were needed to feed a family or protect a homestead." Forestalling further conversation on the subject, he put his hand to his forehead to block the rays of the evening sun. "Through the orchard or around it?"

"Around it. Toward those pines over there."

They settled into silence again as they rode side by side. When they entered a grove of trees, only a few rays of sunlight dappled the ground. The hush under the canopy was broken by the chirping of birds, the brush of branches against each other. The smell of earth was redolent with pine and moss, and they couldn't hear their horses' hooves on the carpet of pine needles. Shannon saw some of the tension leave Rafe's shoulders. This place always did that for her. That's why she'd brought him here.

They heard the ripple of water before they saw it. Finally the pine canopy gave way to scattered maples and cedars and cottonwoods along the edge of the wide creek. There was a meadow to their right with grass as green as spring and dappled with wildflowers in white, yellow and purple. This was a magic place for Shannon.

"How did you find this?" Rafe asked.

"After I bought the Rocky R, I went exploring. When I found this, I knew I belonged here."

He dismounted, tethered his horse to a tree and started toward the meadow.

She dismounted, too, but let him wander ahead of her. He stood in the last rays of sun, his hands dug deep into his jeans pockets as he stared over the water, then high into the trees.

After giving him a few moments alone, she tethered her mount and crossed to Rafe, standing beside him, trying to see what he was seeing.

"I've never ridden like this before," he said.

"What do you mean?"

"Back in Salinas, I rode at Longmeadow Farms. It's a boarding stable, and they have their own horses and give lessons. All of the trails are well marked. There are maps of them back at the stables and never any unexpected discoveries."

"I don't think I could stand a canned trail ride."

He glanced at her. "I guess I didn't know there was any other kind."

Suddenly the sound of a helicopter hummed in the distance.

When Rafe glanced up at the sky, Shannon explained, "The chopper belongs to one of my neighbors. He helps with search and rescue in the mountains."

The faraway noise reminded Rafe that no place was sacred anymore, yet this place came close. Shannon fit in so perfectly out here. She was as natural as the trees and wildflowers. For the first time he realized she reminded him of a pioneer woman. At least her spirit did. She wasn't afraid to use her hands to work hard or to get her hair mussed by a breeze. So different from Nancy.

His wife couldn't be without the cosmetics in her dressing room. She wouldn't think of leaving the house without perfectly manicured nails or sprayed with perfume that cost a small fortune. She didn't like driving with the windows down in the car because the air would toss her hair. When she went swimming, she was a bathing beauty beside the pool, never in it. She couldn't abide the smell of chlorine on her skin. Although she'd had a model-thin figure, she hadn't liked exercise of any kind because she hated to sweat. He'd suspected she'd only agreed to go riding with him because there was a social crowd who were patrons of the stable that gave prestigious parties. She liked being with them...liked showing up in her expensive riding habit and getting compliments...liked standing next to the horses and having her picture taken.

Abruptly he cut off all the thoughts. He felt as if he was betraying what he'd felt for her, seeing her idiosyncrasies as flaws, comparing them to qualities he found in Shannon that intrigued and attracted him. Each day he spent at the Rocky R, he enjoyed learning something new about her, and that disconcerted him.

"We'd better start back," he said curtly.

"I thought we could walk along the stream for a while—"

"I don't want Janine to think I deserted her."

"What's wrong, Rafe?"

When he looked into Shannon's beautiful brown eyes, he felt even more unsettled. "Nothing's wrong."

"One minute everything was peaceful. You were relaxed—"

"Don't try to analyze me. Janine's your patient. I'm not."

Shannon took a step back, and a hurt look came into her eyes. It couldn't be, could it? A woman like her would have a tough hide. Wouldn't she?

If he *had* seen hurt, it wasn't there for long. Shannon brushed her hair back and squared her shoulders. "No, you're not my client. But how you act, what you do, what you think and what you feel *does* affect Janine."

"I already told you I know I'm the reason she's not talking."

"I still don't think that's true. She has to come to terms with what happened to her, but you do, too."

"I have."

"You haven't," she argued. "You're angry about what happened, and you have every right to be. But at some point you're going to have to let go of the anger."

He'd thought he'd hidden it so well. He'd thought he'd covered it with patience. He'd thought he'd pushed it aside so he could help his daughter. Shannon saw too clearly, and he didn't like that at all. "When I get my daughter back, then I'll stop feeling as if fate is an underhanded, dirty dealer."

Although Shannon's voice was compassionate, her words were direct. "Janine might never be the little girl she was before your wife died. You have to be prepared for that."

"I'm not. I brought her here so you could get her over this."

"And I'll do my best. But everything that happens to us changes us a little. What happened to Janine changed her a lot. It changed you, too."

"How do you know?" he growled.

"Intuition."

He scoffed at that. Shannon Collins thought she knew so much. He'd learned very young not to let anyone really know him—certainly not his mother, who was more interested in her boyfriends than him, definitely not the foster families who took him in and didn't care what he did or who he became. He realized now, Nancy hadn't really known him, either. She'd seen him as her protector. She'd looked to him for everything she'd needed. Because of that he'd constantly played the role of White Knight, never letting her see the chinks in his armor.

Turning away from Shannon and the field of wildflowers, he walked back to his horse. When he began Shannon's pavilion in a few days, he would hammer out his anger and his frustrations. The sheer physical exertion would get his mind off Shannon Collins and the bedlam inside him that she caused.

In her office checking notes on her clients' chart at noon the following day, Shannon heard the phone ring and knew Cora would get it. She was having enough trouble keeping her mind on her work without interruptions.

I'm not your patient. Janine is.

She'd felt unreasonably hurt at Rafe's words last night. She'd tried to put that hurt aside, but she couldn't forget about it. It was obvious he didn't want her to get close. It was obvious he'd put up protective walls that weren't coming down anytime soon.

Usually Cora buzzed Shannon if she needed to take the call, but now her aunt came to stand in the doorway of her office. "It's Mr. Donneker, and he doesn't sound happy," Cora warned her.

Shannon had hoped Jordy Donneker would call to make an appointment to see her so they could discuss the progress his daughter had and hadn't made in therapy. She had a feeling he wasn't calling to make an appointment.

"Hello, Mr. Donneker," she said pleasantly.

"I want my money back."

"Mr. Donneker, if you would come to the Rocky R so we could talk about this—"

"There's nothing to talk about. I brought Krissie to you because her teacher told me you could help her get her grades up. Well, she got all Cs and Ds on her report card. That's not gettin' 'em up."

Krissie Donneker was nine years old. When she'd come to Shannon in March, she'd been afraid of her own shadow. In Shannon's estimation, that was due to Jordy Donneker's outbursts, his critical attitude and lack of skills as a single parent. Shannon had hoped to eventually persuade him to come into counseling with his daughter, though she knew that would be a hard sell. After discussing Krissie with her teacher, Shannon had realized the nine-year-old's poor grades were more a result of her unhappiness at home than any difficulty in learning. She'd only seen Krissie once every two weeks for three months, but Shannon had felt they were making progress in confidence building. Although her final grades hadn't improved much, her teacher had told Shannon that she saw a change in

Krissie and the way she related to the other students. She was friendlier, less tentative, was responding more in class without being prodded.

"We need to discuss the progress Krissie *did* make," Shannon said firmly.

"I ain't seen no progress. I don't have money to spend on her coming to you and playing with horses. It's not like we have an insurance that covers it. As far as I'm concerned, you took me across, and I want my money back. You don't give it to me, and I'm going to hire myself a lawyer."

To Shannon's frustration and dismay, he hung up.

When she put down the receiver, she knew Jordy Donneker wasn't making empty threats. In his mind, she'd cheated him.

Should she just give him his money back?

She leaned back in her desk chair with a sigh. If she did that, she'd be setting a precedent. She had insurance for this type of thing....

She knew *she* should consult a lawyer.

A thought entered her head. Rafe was a lawyer.

Yes, he was. But she suspected he didn't want to get involved in her life any more than he wanted her involved in his.

Shannon glanced up at the clock on the wall. She had an hour and a half before her next client arrived. Lunchtime was catch as catch can on the Rocky R. Cora kept the refrigerator stocked. Rafe and Janine usually ate at the house, and Shannon grabbed whatever she could on the run. Sometimes she had back-to-back clients and no time for more than sunflower seeds and an apple.

But today she needed peace and quiet more than

she needed lunch. There was only one way to really get that.

Taking her hat from the rack on the wall, she set it on her head, letting the strap dangle under her chin. She stopped at Cora's desk to tell her, "I'm going for a ride."

"Too much on your plate?"

"You know me too well," Shannon said with affection in her voice.

"I know you bite off more than you can chew. You always have. You don't have to prove anything to anyone, honey."

Cora's words made Shannon's throat tighten. As a little girl, she'd thought if she was good enough, if she could do everything well enough, then maybe her dad would love her. Maybe he'd stop yelling. Maybe he'd stop punching. For a moment Cora's words brought it all back, and she took a deep breath. She hadn't thought about any of this for years. Again she asked herself, *Why now?*

"I need to clear my head and figure out the best way to handle everything," she explained vaguely to her aunt.

"Including having a stranger under your roof?"

"Especially that."

Before Cora could ask any more questions or probe too deeply, Shannon went to the corral and gave a loud whistle. Gray Lady tossed her head up and came running from the pasture toward Shannon, tail flying. Shannon saddled her horse quickly, knowing her time was limited if she wanted to ride out to the meadow by the creek and get back for her next appointment. But that's where she needed to go. She needed to sit in the middle of those flowers with the sunshine pouring down on her. Some people took showers to clear their heads. Others took long walks. She went and sat in the meadow.

As Shannon crossed the terrain she and Rafe had traveled the evening before, she tried not to think about him but kept her attention on her surroundings. The knee-high corn, the long grass, golden in the midday sun, the scent of honeysuckle and sun-warmed earth were pleasant and familiar. She was looking up at the expanse of wonderfully blue sky when she heard the hum of a helicopter in the distance again. But this chopper didn't stay in the distance.

The sound grew louder and louder until Gray Lady slowed to a stop in spite of Shannon urging her forward. Shannon patted the mare on the neck. "It's okay. It'll be gone soon."

The mare didn't like the idea of the big machine coming anywhere near her and she skittered sideways.

Shannon thought about dismounting, but knew the hum wouldn't last much longer. She urged Lady forward again, and the mare started walking reluctantly.

As the helicopter hovered above them at its loudest, Shannon caught movement out of the corner of her eye and saw a fox practically leap from a grove of almonds directly in front of the skittish horse. Lady reared up and Shannon fell to the ground hard on her shoulder.

The fall knocked the wind out of her, and before she could get her breath back, Lady was running from the sound of the chopper as well as from the fox, leaving Shannon on the ground and filled with dismay. She called after her horse, but her voice was lost. When she pushed herself to a sitting position, her left shoulder hurt and she rubbed it.

Checking her watch, she hurriedly got to her feet. Even if she walked fast she wouldn't be back at the ranch by her next appointment. Suddenly she felt dizzy and she sat back down again, dropping her head between her knees. She was just shaken up, she told herself. She'd be fine in a few minutes, and then she'd start back.

Still about a mile and a half from the ranch, Shannon saw Rafe riding toward her with Gray Lady in tow. She should be thrilled to see him, but she knew she looked a mess. She was sweating profusely under her hat and her T-shirt was sticking to her, damp with sweat. Her jeans were dusty from the fall. And her hair? She just wouldn't take her hat off, that was all.

With a relieved expression on his face, Rafe rode closer, and she could feel his gaze raking her up and down.

"I'm fine," she said before he could ask. Yet her voice was a lot weaker than she would like it to be.

After he dismounted, he took a bottle of water from his saddlebag and came toward her, handing it to her. "Drink," he ordered.

She took the bottle gratefully and swallowed at least a quarter of it while Lady brushed her nose against Shannon's arm as if apologizing for running off.

When Shannon stopped drinking and patted Lady's neck, telling her she forgave her, Rafe asked, "What happened?"

"Lady spooked when a helicopter hovered overhead and a fox ran out in front of her."

"You really are all right?" He was frowning and checking her over again.

"Just had the wind knocked out of me. Let's get going. I've got clients to see."

He caught her elbow. It was the side she'd fallen on, and she winced when she felt the tug on her shoulder.

"You're *not* fine."

"I'm just a little sore. Really, Rafe. Just hot and thirsty and feeling like a fool."

"You're no fool, Shannon. This could have happened to anyone."

"I hope everyone isn't worried."

"We *were* worried. But Cora reminded me before I left that you can take care of yourself. I promised Janine I'd find you...or Lady would," he added with a small smile.

Even though she was sore and hot, she couldn't ignore the quickening in her body when she looked up at Rafe. "We've got to get back," she said again, and this time moved quickly toward Lady's side before he could stop her.

His legs were longer than hers, and he was beside her in an instant. "I'll help you up. You probably don't want to pull on that shoulder."

He was close enough behind her that she could feel his body heat. She put her foot in the stirrup and took hold of the saddle's pommel with her good hand, intending not to need Rafe...intending to do this herself. But she simply couldn't do it one-handed. When she tried to pull herself up with both, her shoulder did hurt. He must have seen her wince, because his hands were on her bottom, and then he was boosting her up, and she was on top of the horse before she knew it—with the imprint of his palm burned into her jeans.

She looked down at him. "Now you need a Stetson," she mumbled.

"Why?"

"Because you're acting like a real cowboy." She couldn't help but smile at him.

"The next time we go into town, I'll see what I can do about that." And he smiled back.

She could count the number of times she'd seen Rafe *really* smile. It practically made her bones melt. She turned serious then and kept her gaze steady on his. "Thank you for coming to find me. You must have remembered everything about our ride last night."

"I remembered," he responded simply, and everything about their conversation came back to her again…everything that she'd ridden out here to forget.

She broke eye contact and took hold of her reins. When Rafe stepped away from Lady, she guided her horse toward the Rocky R, not any clearer now on what she should do about Jordy Donneker—or about Rafe.

As they rode back to the ranch, Rafe kept a watchful eye on Shannon. Just because she'd said she was fine, didn't mean she was. He suspected that shoulder might be hurting her more than she was letting on. He'd never met a woman as gutsy as she was and again wondered what had made her that way. After he'd found her, he'd wanted to gather her into his arms and kiss her until he forgot how worried he'd been when her dappled gray mare had come back to the Rocky R alone. Not kissing Shannon again was an endurance test, and he didn't know how much longer he could hold out.

Shannon nudged her horse into a faster pace and

then slowed. He'd bet his boots her shoulder hurt when it was jostled.

As they arrived at the corral, Cora, Clancy and Janine came over to them. Shannon didn't wait for Rafe to help her dismount, and he'd expected that.

"I'm fine," she said quickly to Cora and Clancy with a smile, but then went over to Janine and knelt down before her. "Were you worried about me?" Shannon asked the little girl.

Janine stood perfectly still.

"My horse heard noises she didn't like. Then a fox ran out in front of her, scaring her. When she reared up, I fell off. I was walking back when your dad found me. I'm glad he did, because it's a very long walk."

After studying Shannon's face for a few moments, Janine threw her arms around Shannon's neck and hugged her hard. Immediately Shannon returned the hug, holding the little girl securely.

The scene tightened Rafe's chest. There was a bond forming between Janine and Shannon. Not only that, his daughter had shown more emotion in the past week than she had in the past eighteen months. That was real progress, as far as he was concerned. Maybe this therapy was going to work after all.

After Shannon stood, Cora informed her, "Michelle Lawrence and her mother waited a half hour, and then left. Agnes Broney brought Artie about ten minutes ago and they're waiting in your office."

"I have back-to-back clients today. I'd better get over there. I'll call Michelle's mother myself later and reschedule her appointment. Can you get me a clean T-shirt from the house, and one of my ponytail bands?"

"Sure can." Cora glanced down at Janine. "Do you want to come with me?"

The little girl nodded, followed Cora to the house, with Buster trotting along beside them.

Shannon had turned toward her office when Rafe said, "You really should put some ice on your shoulder."

But she just shook her head. "I don't have time for that now. I'll do it later." Then her brown eyes locked to his. "Thanks again for finding me."

Deep in his heart Rafe knew Shannon Collins didn't accept help often, and certainly didn't need a rescuer. Truth be told, he'd gotten tired of being Nancy's white knight. But he'd liked giving Shannon a hand today. And he suddenly knew she would do the same thing for him. "No problem," he muttered, and then added, "and I'll look for that Stetson when I go into town."

At that she smiled and then took off toward her office.

Clancy was standing by the corral. Going over to the boy, Rafe knew there was one more thing he could do for Shannon. "Shannon fell on her shoulder today. It'll probably be even more sore by evening, though she won't admit it."

Clancy gave an understanding nod. "I'll make sure all the stalls are clean so she doesn't have to do it. I'll get all the horses in and fed, too." There was no sullenness about Clancy now, just a willingness to help a woman he apparently admired.

"I'll give you a hand," Rafe offered.

Clancy looked surprised but didn't object.

Rafe and Clancy completed the chores before Shannon finished with her last client in the corral. A man in a red SUV picked up Clancy. Jim Brenneman introduced himself to Rafe through his open car window. He looked to be in his sixties, had thinning brown hair and was congenial and pleasant. Again Rafe wondered about Clancy's story.

At supper a half hour later, Rafe noticed Shannon wasn't moving her shoulder. ''Did you put ice on that yet?'' he asked her as they cleared the table after the meal.

''I'm going to get a shower now. Then I will. Thanks for helping Clancy finish up the chores. I appreciate it.''

''I figured you might.'' He wanted to kiss her, yet he knew they'd both be better off if he didn't.

After Rafe went outside, he saw Janine was dividing her attention between watching Cora do needlework on the swing on the front porch and playing with a kitten. He caught the whiff of roses growing along the side of the house. After the day that Shannon had had, maybe she would appreciate a few flowers. He still felt guilty about what he'd said to her last night. Though it was true, he hadn't intended to sound so harsh.

After finding some scissors in the kitchen, he cut two red roses and a delicate yellow one, added a few fern fronds and took them into the kitchen intending to look for something to put them in.

Instead, he found Shannon with the freezer door open. She was wearing a turquoise-and-white terry cloth romper. It molded to her breasts, laid seductively over her hips, showed off her beautifully curved legs. His blood ran fast and his pulse sped up.

Shannon removed an ice pack from the freezer and shut the door. Then she saw him standing there, the flowers in his hand.

"These are for you," he said huskily, wanting to stroke her beautiful curly hair, wanting to kiss her until they both forgot everything that was wrong with the world.

Shannon slowly put the ice pack on the counter and took the flowers from him. Then she did something that he never expected to see Shannon do.

She cried!

Chapter Seven

Shannon's dark-brown eyes glistened as she fought valiantly for control.

A woman's tears didn't affect Rafe much anymore. They'd been common with Nancy. Whenever she'd been scared or upset, she'd let them fall freely, and he would have had to calm her down or console her before they could deal with the problem. He'd also dealt with theatrical tears and desperate ones with witnesses. But Shannon's tears twisted his gut because he guessed they were rare.

"Hey," he said gently as one slid down her cheek. "This wasn't the effect I was going for."

"Sorry," she murmured, ducking her head and looking down at the flowers.

This woman had gotten up with the sun to do chores, had seen clients until she'd ridden off on her horse and been thrown, walked about forty-five minutes in the midday sun with her body aching and had then returned to her professional duties for the rest of the day, hardly taking a breath. If anyone deserved to let off a little stress, she did. He couldn't help wrapping his arms around her and bringing her close to his chest, flowers and all.

For a few moments he felt resistance, then with a sigh she laid her head against his shoulder.

His chin settled in her hair as if it belonged there, and he said in a low voice, ''You've had a very long day.''

The click of the ceramic teapot clock on the wall was the only sound in the kitchen. Shannon's silky curls brushed over the top of Rafe's hand, and his fingertips tingled as he realized how much he wanted to stroke them. Stroke her. Her terry cloth romper felt like less than a towel between their lower bodies. One of her thighs was pressed against his. The scent of the roses and greens between them reminded him why she was in his arms. He wanted it to be for another reason—not one of gratitude, but because she needed him as much as he needed her.

Without unwrapping his arm from around her, he took the flowers from her hand and laid them on the counter.

''Rafe...'' The word was a plea and a protest.

As she looked up at him, the certainty of what he was going to do was mirrored in her liquid brown eyes. He wanted to hold on to the anticipation of kissing her again. He wanted to hold on to the arousal that made him believe he was alive again. He wanted to hold on to Shannon until he took her someplace private...someplace where they could explore each other and forget responsibilities—experience only pleasure.

When he bent his head slowly, he felt her tense as if she was preparing herself. But she didn't pull away. She just kept looking at him with as many questions as he had. He was ignoring them and hoped she would, too, at least for a few minutes.

This time he didn't take her right away. He rubbed his lips across hers, back and forth, until she parted hers with a soft sigh. He opened his mouth, giving her his breath and taking hers. The sheer sensuality of it fully aroused him. Since she'd just taken a shower, the honeysuckle scent of her soap was strong and intoxicating, winding around him. While Shannon swayed into him, he leaned against the counter to support both of them. A woman's kiss had never made him shake before. What was it about Shannon Collins that pushed every button of his libido…that made him envision sinking into her and having her legs wrap around him?

Just the thought of it made him open his mouth wider over hers so he could explore her more fully. When his tongue delved into her mouth, she grabbed on to him as if her world, too, was spinning.

He realized he wanted elemental and primitive with Shannon—not satin sheets and fake dim lights and slow, increasingly pleasurable arousal. He wanted earth and moon and grass and night. He wanted fast and furious.

Shannon's hands moved restlessly on his shoulders as their tongues mated.

He was getting lost in the thrill of her hands on him when the screen door banged. The sound didn't belong…the sound shattered everything that had been happening between them. Shannon practically jumped away.

He was a bit slower to respond, needing to subjugate his body's desire to his will, needing to take a deep breath and pull himself together before either Cora or his daughter appeared.

Thank goodness it was only Cora who breezed into the kitchen, hardly giving either of them a second glance. "I offered Janine some of that leftover ice cream, and she decided to take me up on it. How about you two?"

Quickly Shannon gathered up her ice bag and the flowers on the counter, her cheeks flushed dark rose. "I'm..." Her voice was whispery, and she tried again. "I'm going to turn in."

Cora set the plastic container of ice cream on the table, then opened an upper cabinet and took out a vase. "You'll need this." She glanced at Rafe. "Ice cream for you?"

He would probably be better off with a cold shower. "Sure." Then he couldn't help taunting Shannon. "If you want a dish, I'll bring it back to you."

For a moment their gazes connected, and he realized she was still living the kiss, too. Her bedroom would have been a great place to take it. But anger flashed in her eyes at his mere suggestion of it. "No, thanks. You enjoy the ice cream with your daughter. I'll see you in the morning."

Her mention of Janine put a barricade between them, and apparently that's exactly what Shannon wanted. Okay, so she wasn't the kind of woman to enjoy flings. But they certainly could have a hell of a good time with one.

After Shannon said good-night to her aunt and left the kitchen, Cora eyed him curiously. "Did I interrupt something?" There was a hint of amusement in her voice.

He felt like a teenager who'd gotten caught necking in someone else's backyard. "Yes, you did," he said honestly.

Cora let out a whoop of a laugh. "Well, good. Maybe next time you two will know to go someplace more private."

The following afternoon, Janine drew a picture at the small table and chairs in Shannon's office while the air-conditioning unit hummed in the background. That morning, as they'd worked with Marigold, Rafe's daughter had seemed distracted. Soon Shannon would try to put Janine on Marigold's back. She wanted to make sure the little girl was ready.

It was getting more and more difficult for Shannon to keep perspective with Janine. Their silent connection was almost more binding than a vocal one. Shannon knew, not only was Janine becoming attached to her, but *she* was becoming attached to Janine. Was that because of her growing feelings for Rafe?

She couldn't be sure. She *was* sure that the slightest thing could trigger Janine's talking again...or send her further into her shell. Just as those flowers last night had touched Shannon so much she hadn't been able to hold back the tears.

How long had it been since she'd actually cried?

How long had it been since she'd kissed a man three times in a week? A man she wasn't even sure she should be getting involved with.

Janine laid down her crayon and pushed the piece of paper toward Shannon.

Rising from her desk, Shannon went over to the small table and sat on one of the little chairs. When she looked at the picture, she knew exactly what it was.

She pointed to a stick drawing of a gray horse. "Is that Gray Lady?"

Janine nodded.

The picture depicted grass and trees and another stick figure that looked broken as it lay on the ground. "Is that me?" Shannon asked.

Janine nodded again.

Shannon had tried to get Janine to write out answers to her questions, but the child had seemed as unwilling to do that as she was to talk. So they relied on this "yes" and "no" system, with Shannon following her instincts and reading between the lines. "Were you scared yesterday when Gray Lady came back without me?"

Janine's eyes grew wide and she gave a small but perceptible nod. Then she stood, as if she'd had enough of all of this, and went to the door, signaling that she wanted to leave.

But Shannon knew it was time to push a little more. "Janine, it's all right to be scared. It's all right to show other people that you're scared. Especially your dad and me."

Janine turned the knob on the door and opened it.

With a sigh Shannon stood, went over to the little girl and crouched down beside her. "If you let me or your dad know how you feel in here—" Shannon tapped Janine's heart "—we can help you be not so scared and not so worried."

After a long look into Shannon's eyes, Janine shrugged and slipped out the door.

Shannon knew all about wanting to escape pain and feelings. In the long run, the escape didn't help. In spite of that, she followed Janine, hoping Marigold was the key. There was something she wanted to try, but she needed Rafe's permission.

As soon as she and Janine stepped outside, she said to her, "Let's go see how your dad's doing with the pavilion."

The lumber had been delivered early that morning, and already Rafe was sawing. He'd said something about mixing up concrete to anchor the support beams later in the day.

She stopped when she spotted him. He'd taken off his shirt. It hung over a cedar about ten feet from him. He needed to do the sawing at the back of the house where the extension cord could reach.

Uninterested in what her dad was doing, Janine ran to the old swing, sat on it and gave herself a push.

Shannon had made conversation with Rafe at breakfast, but she was still embarrassed over what had happened last night. The sight of his furred chest didn't make her feel any more at ease.

When he spied her, he swiped his wrist across his sweaty forehead. "I think I'll take a break until after supper. Is there anyplace around where Janine and I can go swimming?"

"The community center in town has an outdoor pool, but it gets pretty crowded. I don't know how Janine would take to that. If you want privacy, I can show you to our neighbor's pond. You get there by a back road. It's only about a half mile."

"I could keep working now, and we could all go tonight," Rafe suggested with a hint of a smile.

The thought of seeing Rafe in a bathing suit, the thought of her being in a bathing suit anywhere near him, sent shivers up and down her back despite the heat. "I can't go this evening. I'm meeting Nolan for dinner to talk about setting up the press conference."

Rafe eyed her with a scowl. "You're still going to do that?"

"Yes. Nolan's donation will make the indoor ring a reality. I might even be able to have it finished before winter."

Rafe's gaze went to his daughter, who was swinging as easily as any child would. She was gazing up at the sky, trying to touch her toes to the clouds. "Are you seeing progress with Janine?" he asked, as if the thought of an indoor ring had led him to the subject of his daughter's therapy.

Instead of answering, Shannon asked, "Are you?"

His eyes narrowed as he swung his gaze back to hers. "*You're* the therapist, Shannon. I'm asking for your expert opinion."

"And I'm asking for your opinion as a father. Sometimes that counts more."

He took a full, patient breath. "I'm not sure. I think I *feel* a difference, if that makes any sense. For months before we came here, she wouldn't even look at me directly. Now, I catch her smiling. But those things aren't a tangible indication that she's going to talk again anytime soon."

"Those things are a start," Shannon insisted. She'd never told him about coming across Janine giggling with the pony. She didn't want to give him false hope. "You asked for my opinion. I think she *is* making progress. Today when I asked her to draw what was on her mind, she actually did. She was upset about Gray Lady coming back without me. I think her fear was that I wouldn't come back, or that I'd gotten hurt. Up until today, when she drew pictures, they were superficial—things she'd seen around the farm, her house back in Salinas. Getting Janine to talk again is what you want, but there's a lot of healing that has to go on both before *and* after that happens.''

''And you think it is?''

''I think she's letting down her guard, little by little, and she's beginning to trust me.''

''Will she ever trust *me* again?'' he asked, the strain of everything that had happened over the past eighteen months etched around his eyes.

''You've got to give her time. Although you don't think there have been any results from her seeing other therapists, I believe you're wrong about that. Janine's been absorbing and analyzing and thinking all this time. Maybe healing, too. When she feels safe enough, she'll let us all in again. I'd like to videotape her tomorrow, if you don't mind.''

''So you have a case study for your book?'' he asked suspiciously.

''How do you know about my book?''

''Cora mentioned it. And I don't want Janine to be—'' he paused ''—a guinea pig.''

Shannon supposed Rafe's work made him suspicious by nature, but she resented the idea that she'd use Janine's therapy for her own gain. ''I want to videotape Janine to give her a chance to see herself on tape. I want her to see how good she is with Marigold, how she can lead her when she asserts herself, how the pony relates to her. When she sees that, she might understand she has more control over her world than she thinks she does. *That's* why I want to videotape her.''

After he gave Shannon a thoroughly prolonged perusal, he came a few steps closer to her. "Is Janine just another client to you?"

His question took her aback. "What do you mean?"

"She's becoming attached to you, Shannon. I can see that even better than I can see anything else."

"That happens with therapists. If I didn't bond with her, she wouldn't learn to trust me."

"That's all fine and dandy. I just don't want my daughter hurt even more if we leave here because the ranch and horses and you weren't enough."

Shannon squared her shoulders and lifted her chin. Although her attraction to Rafe was more powerful than it had ever been, she ignored it. "Your daughter's well-being is my first priority. If you decide to take her away from here before the therapy has a chance to work, I'll prepare her for that. If anything's going to hurt your daughter, it will be your impatience." Shannon checked her watch as an excuse to end the conversation. "I have to get back to my office."

As she turned to walk away, Rafe's words stopped her. "While you're having dinner with Constantine tonight, just remember nothing in this life is free, Shannon. Not even a donation to a good cause."

Shannon didn't deign to respond. As she walked back toward her office, she wondered if Rafe simply didn't like Nolan, or if he didn't like the idea of her having anything to do with him.

It didn't matter. Rafe would be leaving by August fifth, the deadline he'd set. She was sure of it. When he left, she'd have her work and the Rocky R. What more did she need?

It was almost ten o'clock when Shannon got home that night. Nolan had taken her to dinner at the finest restaurant in town, and their reservations hadn't been until eight. They'd taken their time with coffee afterward. She was glad she'd met Nolan at the restaurant instead of having him pick her up. That way there were no awkward goodbyes. Not that Nolan had been anything more than friendly. They had discussed the press conference and who would be there and what Nolan would say, who Shannon would contact for bids to build the ring and the possibility of finishing it before winter.

Shannon parked her car and went into the house entrance nearest to her room. As she let herself inside, everything was quiet. From outside she hadn't seen lights, so Rafe had probably gone to bed shortly after Janine.

Shannon stopped in her room and stripped off her nylons and dress, pulling her nightshirt over her head. On her way to the kitchen, she didn't hear the hum of the fan upstairs. The heat of the day hadn't cooled much. It would be warm up there.

She turned on a small table lamp in the living room and ascended the stairs by the glow of the night-light in the hall on the second floor. Janine's door was usually open. She didn't want a brighter light to wake her. When Shannon reached the upstairs, she switched on the fan and saw that Rafe's door was open, too. Going to Janine's room, she peeked inside. When she stopped at the foot of the bed, she looked down on the sleeping child and the slumbering dog beside her. Shannon had to smile. Buster would make a terrible watchdog. If a burglar ever tried to break in, he'd sleep through the entire robbery.

Janine looked so peaceful, sleeping on her side, a doll cuddled close to her. Shannon felt much more than she should for one of her clients. She was so tempted to go to the side of the bed, brush Janine's hair from her brow, kiss her on the cheek. She knew what was happening. Janine needed a mother, and *she* longed to *be* a mother. She felt as if she were walking a tightrope. But she had to make sure Janine's interests came first. That meant putting her own needs aside to do what was best for the little girl.

Just like a mother would do, a small voice whispered inside her head.

Lost in that thought, Shannon was startled when she heard a noise come from the room beside Janine's. There was a thump, the creaking of the bed and then another thump.

Rafe's room had been dark, and she'd assumed he was asleep.

Janine and Buster still slept soundly as Shannon went out into the hall, listening carefully. No more thumps, but she heard muttering.

The muttering grew louder and sounded... anguished. She couldn't help peeking into Rafe's room. He was tossing and turning in the bed. He'd knocked a book and notepad off the nightstand. She could make out his words now. "No. Don't shoot!" and she knew he was having a nightmare.

She understood nightmares and how they stole sleep. She'd had them often into her teenage years.

Wanting to help, wanting to end the bad dream for Rafe, she hurried to the side of his bed.

Sweat beaded on his brow, and he tossed and turned.

Without hesitating a moment longer, she gently pressed her hand to his shoulder, feeling the slick sweat on his skin. "Rafe. Rafe, wake up. It's just a dream."

For a moment she thought she might have to shake him harder…might have to physically enter whatever world he was in. Then his eyes flew open, and it only took him an instant to orient himself. "What's wrong? Why are you—"

"I came upstairs to turn on the fan and I heard you. You were having a nightmare."

Grimacing, he pushed himself to a sitting position against the headboard and switched on the bedside lamp. Then he ran his hand through his hair slowly, avoiding her gaze. "It's always the same one," he mumbled.

"Do you want to talk about it?"

He shook his head and gave her a weary look that said he'd been dealing with this for many, many months. "It won't do any good."

"Have you ever told anyone what the nightmare is about?"

"I'm sure not going to inflict it on anybody else."

Nothing could keep her from sitting on the edge of the bed by his knee. "You won't be inflicting anything on me. Tell me what happens in your dream."

Silence grew between them until he took a deep breath, then let it out. "I wasn't at the fast-food restaurant when Nancy was shot, but I saw the pictures of what happened there. A reporter who happened to be nearby was on the scene before the police. He took photographs and—" Rafe just shook his head again. "In the nightmare I'm there. I can see it all happening. But I'm in chains and I can't do anything about it." Sliding his legs over the side of the bed, he picked up the book and notepad that had fallen to the floor, placing them once more on the nightstand.

"Rafe."

His gaze collided with hers then, and she saw the torment there.

"You've got to make the conscious decision to let it go. You've got to forgive yourself for not being there."

His eyes looked haunted. "I don't know if I can ever do that."

She waited, and then he said in a raspy voice, "Some things a man just has to live with."

Shannon wondered if Rafe was holding on to the guilt in order to hold on to his wife.

Moments ticked by until his gaze traveled down Shannon's nightshirt to her knees and bare legs and feet. She was equally aware that he was in his sleeping shorts, and that this was his bedroom. She'd been foolish to come in, but she couldn't stand to see him suffer...

"How was your dinner with Constantine?" he asked abruptly.

There was an edge to Rafe's voice and she proceeded carefully. "Fine. The press conference is going to be on Monday."

"So soon?"

"Nolan has already set it up tentatively with the TV station."

"I see. And you're going to let him use you like this?"

She should have known better than to discuss Nolan's donation with Rafe again. She knew how he felt. "It's a small price to pay to get the ring built. Life's about trade-offs."

His brows arched. "I think the dreamer has a practical side."

When he called her a dreamer, it didn't sound like a compliment. "I'm sure you deal with trade-offs every day in your job. That's what plea agreements are all about, aren't they?"

"What do you know about plea agreements?" he asked with wry amusement.

"Not a lot. But you want criminals behind bars, and sometimes you have to cut a deal to get them there. We can't always get what we want. Sometimes, to get even part of it, we have to take what we can get."

"A half loaf is better than none?"

"Sometimes."

"What if Constantine decides this donation is going to get him more than friendship with you?"

"He'd be wrong. He can have his picture taken in front of the building and next to the plaque as often as he wants, but that's the extent of what his donation will get him. At least as far as I'm concerned."

Rafe studied her steadily, then asked, "You said your engagement ended because you were spending too much time at the Rocky R. Is that the only reason?"

Chapter Eight

Whenever Shannon was around Rafe, tumultuous feelings seemed to sweep her away. Because of that, her defenses crumbled. Now she realized how perceptive he had to be in his job. He'd probably honed his intuition as finely as she'd honed hers and could see deeper than a surface excuse. She'd never discussed her broken engagement with anyone, not even Aunt Cora.

But in the face of Rafe's question, she thought it was important to confide in him. Why? So he'd understand what she was all about? Did she want him to know her as no other man ever had?

Looking directly into Rafe's green eyes, she took a deep breath, then plunged in. "Allen changed once we were engaged. My radar's usually pretty good with men, but for whatever reason, I misread Allen. Once he slipped that ring on my finger, he wanted to make all my decisions for me. Suddenly the wedding was about everything *he* wanted, even the dress. He insisted on going along to look at them, and he kept picking out these…these tulle and lace and taffeta creations that belong on a debutante. After that, it was all downhill.''

Although Rafe's expression didn't change, his eyes seemed to become a deeper green and much too knowing. Now she did look away, studying the wallpaper pattern straight ahead of her. ''I wanted the ceremony in the little church we went to last Sunday. He wanted it in a huge one in Sacramento. I wanted a simple reception here at the Rocky R. He wanted to rent a ballroom. And it wasn't even about our differences. It was about him taking complete control and expecting me to follow. He didn't hear me when I tried to talk to him about it. Just brushed away my concerns with an I-know-best attitude.''

''Why didn't *you* break off the engagement?''

Rafe's voice brought her gaze to him again, and her heart thudded harder. ''I think I would have eventually. But the idea of a family and having children was so very important to me. Still, I was spending a lot of time here, choosing horses, building up my clientele. Pulling away from him was my way of ending it, I guess.''

When Rafe shifted toward her and their knees grazed each other's, she felt naked and vulnerable. She'd fought against feeling vulnerable ever since she'd been a child. With Rafe…feeling vulnerable was terrifying yet in some ways seemed right, too. His hand came up, and she knew he was going to touch her. She wanted him to touch her.

He pushed some curls behind her ear, then ran his

fingers through them. "You're an independent woman, Shannon. I like that. I like your spirit and your strength."

His fingers in her hair were immobilizing her. She might not want any man to control her, but at this moment Rafe had complete control. And she didn't care.

A wry smile slid across Rafe's lips. "I can't seem to stay away from you."

"I can't stay away from you." Her voice was a whisper.

His large hand slid to her nape and nudged her toward him. "Then we'd better do something about it."

The heat emanating from Rafe's body seemed to become her heat. Anticipating his lips on hers, she felt her pulse race.

He didn't kiss her right away. First he asked, "Do you want me to kiss you?"

He was making this her decision, too. He was giving her the freedom to back away. That was the last thing she wanted to do. "Yes," she breathed.

His lips were hot with desire and heat and hunger. As his tongue pushed into her mouth, it was greedy and searching and thoroughly seductive. She'd said yes to the kiss and now she reveled in it…reveled in sliding her hands over his shoulders, feeling the curling hair on his chest as it brushed against her fingers. She didn't think she had ever felt anything as erotic. This wasn't just a kiss. It was an awakening. She'd never known an ache this deep or a desire this strong to know a man and have him know her.

As Rafe's fervor increased, he laid her down on the bed in the midst of the tangled covers at the foot. Her nightshirt had ridden up her thighs, and now Rafe's hand slid beneath it, pushing it up farther. She was amazed by her lack of self-consciousness with him. As his hand found her breasts, all she could think about was touching him as intimately. She cupped his hard arousal, and his deep groan told her she was pleasuring him as much as he was pleasuring her.

"I can forget any nightmare when you do that to me," he growled.

Forget.

That word stood out above all the rest to Shannon. He wanted to forget his nightmare. He wanted to forget his pain. He just wanted to forget and lose himself in pleasure.

Shannon wanted so much more than to forget. She wanted to vault into the future and dreams and hope. At that moment she realized she was falling in love with Rafe; he could become her life.

The thought splashed over her as coldly as the knowledge that he'd be leaving. He had a career and a life in Salinas. What had she been thinking? What had she been doing? What *was* she doing?

She snatched away her hand as if the touch of him burned her. Then she pushed against his shoulder.

He felt the tensing of her body, the urgent push of her fingers against his skin. "What is it?" His voice was raspy with unfulfilled need.

"We've got to stop. I don't just want to be a means for you to 'forget.'"

A dark flush rode high on his cheekbones. He gazed into her eyes steadily for a few heartbeats, and then he pushed himself up and sat on the edge of the bed. "Get out of here, Shannon."

"Rafe…"

"Don't tell me you want to talk about it. Don't tell

me you should have never come in here. And don't
tell me we'll forget about all of this in the morning.''
He shot a frustrated look at her. ''Because we won't.
You have too much good sense for both of us, and I
don't want to be reminded about that now. So go to
bed. The next time I have a nightmare, just leave me
to it.''

The knowledge of her growing feelings for Rafe
rocked her as much as what had almost happened.
With all the dignity she could muster, she pulled her
nightshirt down over her hips and then slid off of the
bed.

She didn't look back as she left his room. She
couldn't. Because if she did, she might forget she had
any good sense at all.

As she descended the steps, she decided that good
sense was highly overrated.

On Monday morning Rafe headed for the barn while
Janine had her session with Shannon. He'd managed
to stay away from Shannon the past few days. She'd
seen him at his worst the night he'd had that damned
nightmare. On top of that, his hunger for her was driving him nuts. The odd thing was that talking to her
after she'd wakened him had seemed right somehow.
He couldn't imagine ever confiding in Nancy like that.
With her he'd had to be strong twenty-four hours a
day, seven days a week. With Shannon...

It hadn't been difficult keeping his distance from
Shannon. Her clients kept her busy on Friday. Saturday afternoon he'd taken Janine into Fawn Grove to
a movie. When they'd seen a family restaurant that
wasn't crowded, they'd gone in for an early supper.

Yesterday had been a bit more difficult. He'd let

Janine sleep late, then they'd made brunch while Shannon and Cora attended church. Later in the day he'd driven Janine into Sacramento, and they'd visited Fairytale Town and the zoo. They'd made a supper of hot dogs and French fries he'd bought from a streetside vendor. He'd found himself talking to Janine as Shannon often did, not expecting a vocal answer but looking for a less obvious one.

As they had since Friday, at breakfast this morning he and Shannon had related like polite strangers. That wasn't what he wanted. Most of the time he was around her, his physical need made him feel like a horse with a burr under his saddle. Shannon had made it clear that she wasn't interested in a one-night stand. The problem was—he couldn't give more.

Rounding the corner of the barn, Rafe smelled cigarette smoke. The next instant he saw where it was coming from. Clancy was lounging against a few bales of hay stacked near the door that opened into the main part of the barn, pitchfork beside him, and there was a lit cigarette in his hand.

Clancy flushed guiltily when he spotted Rafe, but he didn't attempt to hide what he was doing. The defiance was there again.

"You should know better than to smoke a cigarette anywhere near the barn." Rafe nodded to the hay bales.

"It's none of your business what I do," Clancy retorted.

"Does Shannon know you smoke?"

Clancy shrugged. "Maybe she does, maybe she doesn't."

"Do you want me to tell her I caught you smoking

out here?'' As they stared at each other, Rafe could feel their battle of wills.

''I don't care what you tell her,'' Clancy finally mumbled, as he snuffed out the cigarette on the sole of his boot.

Rafe held out his hand for the butt.

''I'll take care of it,'' Clancy snapped, jamming it into his jeans pocket.

''Better douse it, or you'll ruin good jeans.''

Grabbing the pitchfork, Clancy shot Rafe a glance. ''I don't need a keeper.''

Rafe knew that's exactly what Clancy did need. ''Do your parents know you smoke?''

''I don't have parents.''

''I thought I heard Cora say your dad was picking you up at four.''

''He's my *foster* dad.''

Rafe knew all too well about foster parents. Yet he'd met Jim Brenneman, the man he'd thought was Clancy's father. He seemed kind and caring and concerned about the teenager under his care. ''Do you have a foster mom, too?''

Clancy nodded.

''How long have you lived with the Brennemans?''

Clancy gave Rafe a ''what's it to you'' look, but then answered him. ''Two years.'' Grabbing a pitchfork, Clancy made it clear the get-to-know-you session was over. ''I have to get back to my chores.'' But before he moved away, he asked, ''Are you going to tell Shannon about the smoking?''

Rafe thought about it a moment. ''Not this time.''

''Why not?'' Clancy asked curiously.

''Because I think everybody deserves a second chance.''

"If you want to tell, you go ahead and tell. I don't care."

There was something in Clancy's eyes that said he *did* care. The boy was filled with bravado, which saved his pride but might get him into trouble. Before Rafe could ask any more questions or give a lecture, Clancy quickly headed around the corner of the barn toward the stalls.

Rafe went inside the barn and crossed to the tack room and his toolbox, knowing he saw himself in Clancy. At that age he'd been stubborn and defiant and known better than the rest of the world, too.

Around one o'clock, Rafe was in the kitchen returning the mustard and margarine to the refrigerator when he saw Nolan Constantine's white Cadillac roll in. He was there in plenty of time to set the scene for the press conference. Rafe was tempted to disappear until Constantine and the news crew had gone, but he was curious about the whole thing, too. This morning at breakfast, Shannon had explained to Janine, "There will be many different people here on the Rocky R this afternoon." She'd told his daughter about the lights and the cameras and the microphones.

Rafe had offered Janine the choice of leaving the Rocky R during the news conference or staying down at the corral. The cameras would be set up on the front porch of the house. Janine had pointed to the corral. There was no doubt about it. She loved being with Marigold and the kittens and Buster—and everything the ranch had to offer.

Rafe found himself liking all of it as well. Maybe too much. He'd always thought he was a city person, but life out here offered different advantages—some that seemed to soothe his soul. He'd like to continue working on the pavilion during the press conference, but there was nothing to keep Janine busy up there while he was doing that.

A half hour later as his daughter groomed Marigold, Rafe replaced a few of the rotting boards in the pony's shed. The small structure needed a good coat of paint, too. He'd see to that after he finished the pavilion.

While he was hammering nails into place, the news van pulled in, followed by a string of other cars. Constantine must have invited every reporter in Sacramento and Fawn Grove, Rafe thought wryly.

As the time neared three o'clock, Cora appeared with a thermos of iced tea. Rafe poured himself a paper cupful and drank it. "Thanks. That's just what I needed."

Janine was sitting in the grass, using a long blade of dried hay to tease a gray-and-white kitten into playing. Buster sat on his haunches watching curiously, as if he couldn't understand what the kitten was doing.

Cora leaned her head toward Janine. "I'll keep an eye on her if you want to see what's going on up at the house. The press conference is about to start."

"You think I'm interested?" he asked in a bland tone.

Cora crossed her arms over her chest and pinned him with her direct, brown gaze. "You're darn tootin' you're interested. Everything that girl does interests you, and vice versa. My bones might creak, but my eyesight's still twenty-twenty. Just because you two dance around each other and pretend there's nothing going on, doesn't mean nothing's going on."

He'd thought he'd done admirably well over the weekend, acting like a noninvolved houseguest. "Do you always say exactly what's on your mind?"

"Sure do. I'll never get an ulcer that way."

He shook his head and drank the rest of his iced tea. "Is Clancy up at the news conference?"

"Yep. All those cameras and wires and stuff fascinated him. His dad's picking him up at four."

"He told me today Jim's his foster father."

"That he is. A good man, too. And his wife Marge is a nice lady. Clancy could have done a lot worse."

"Clancy works here to make extra money?"

"Not exactly."

"What, exactly?"

With a shrug Cora said, "Most people in town know what happened with Clancy, so I guess it won't hurt to tell you. He tried to shoplift that pair of boots he's wearin'. Bob Coulson was havin' a sale at his store, boxes were stacked up everywhere, and I guess Clancy thought he could get away with it. But Bob's no fool. He caught the boy not five feet from his front door."

Cora poured Janine a cup of tea. "Jim didn't want to see the boy start life with a record, and he wanted Bob to let Clancy work for him to earn the money to pay off the boots. Bob didn't like that idea. Jim knew about Shannon's work out here, and he knew Clancy liked horses, though he'd never had much chance to be around them. So he called Shannon, and after she had a talk with Clancy she decided he could be a big help on the Rocky R. He could pay off the boots and then stay on to earn extra money if he wanted."

"She wants to save the world, doesn't she?" Rafe asked, with part admiration, part exasperation.

Smiling at him, the older woman nodded. "Her part of it, anyway. Mostly, she just does what she can with what God's given her. That's really what most people try to do.''

After thinking about it, Rafe decided he *would* like to see how Shannon handled herself at this press conference. He had a feeling he knew how Nolan Constantine would handle *himself*.

By the time Rafe washed up at the outside spigot, then crossed the lane and covered the grassy area in front of the house, Constantine was at the microphone making a speech.

Standing beside him, Shannon had dressed for the occasion. Still casual, but very much the professional therapist, she was wearing a royal-blue sleeveless sweater over slacks of the same shade. Since he'd done his own share of press conferences, he knew blue looked good on TV. Constantine had probably clued her in.

Nolan Constantine's voice rang out. ''Shannon Collins's therapy helps children live full, rich lives again. She works energetically to—''

Suddenly Constantine's speech was interrupted. A tall, reed-thin man with glasses, in a T-shirt, jeans, a Stetson and boots, leaped to the mike and grabbed it from Constantine's hands. He pointed one bony finger at Shannon for the camera to follow and said into the mike, ''She doesn't help kids. What she does is quackery. I brought my daughter to her to help, and she didn't. She just took my money. And she won't give it back. Is that fair? My insurance doesn't cover her therapy, and I'll bet a lot of other people's doesn't, either. Do they know they're just throwing their money away?''

Shannon went white.

Blustering all over the place, Constantine reached for the mike, but the man wouldn't hand it back.

The reporter—a pretty blonde in her twenties, whose station was taping the press conference—stepped in like any good reporter would. "And what is your name, sir?"

Rafe took a few steps closer to the front, just in case the man got nasty.

"Jordy Donneker."

"You say your daughter came to Shannon Collins for therapy?" the reporter asked.

"She came for three months, and I didn't see any change in her. None. Her grades were supposed to go up. Well, they didn't. She has to go to summer school."

Trying to be fair, the blonde asked, "Don't you think you might have given Dr. Collins more time?"

"I don't have money to be throwin' away." He looked over the crowd and pointed at Rafe. "I saw you and your daughter come in to the Twin Pines on Saturday. The waitress told me your kid can't talk and you're staying out here. Is Dr. Collins helping her, yet?"

Rafe knew everyone in a town the size of Fawn Grove knew everyone's business. They especially knew about strangers or outsiders. When he and Janine had gone into town on Saturday and had supper at the family restaurant, he'd felt the waitress and a woman behind the counter eyeing them and even consulting at one point. He imagined the scuttlebutt. "They're staying at Shannon Collins's place." "His daughter can't talk."

But whether Fawn Grove's grapevine was buzzing about him and Janine or not, he didn't intend to discuss his private concerns in public. Especially not in front of a TV camera. Thank goodness Janine had stayed back at the corral.

"I don't discuss my daughter in public," Rafe stated firmly.

"So don't discuss her," Donneker snapped. "Just tell us if you've seen any improvement. Have you seen anything that makes you think this therapy is going to work?"

When Rafe still remained silent, Donneker came at him again. "Is your daughter talking yet?"

"No, she's not," Rafe had to finally admit. "But that doesn't mean she won't. I've seen small signs—"

"What kind of signs?" the reporter asked with interest.

"The way her eyes meet mine. Her demeanor."

But Donneker brushed his observations away. "That's a bunch of hogwash Shannon Collins probably pointed out to you. The bottom line is, she's not talking."

Using the courtroom calm he'd honed since he'd passed the bar, Rafe kept his voice even but firm. "Mr. Donneker, whether my daughter is talking yet or not is none of your business. Besides that, you're on private property. Shannon Collins's property. If you continue to slander her in public, you'd better find yourself a good lawyer."

Donneker's eyes flashed angrily as he took an even more defensive stance with his fists balled. "I've *got* a lawyer. *Dr. Collins's* the one who better find a lawyer. I have first-amendment rights. I can say anything I please."

"*I'm* a lawyer, Mr. Donneker," Rafe informed the man. "Dr. Collins has the right to have you removed from her property, if she so wishes. If you think you have grounds for a legal suit, then you put it in writing instead of making threats. If you don't leave now, I'll call the police and they can escort you from the property.''

Donneker glared at him and then at Shannon. Thrusting the mike back at Constantine, he said loud enough for everyone to hear, ''I'll leave. I got my point across. I just better see it on the eleven o'clock news, or I'll know you're censoring it for the sake of somebody who's got lots of money.'' It was obvious he meant Nolan Constantine, and Rafe thought the situation couldn't get any stickier.

After Donneker strode to his pickup truck, he climbed in quickly and took off with a squeal of tires and a cloud of dust.

To his credit, Constantine picked up the mike and smiled at his audience. Falling back into his philanthropic role, he said easily, ''Shannon Collins's credentials are impeccable. There is a long list of children she's helped.''

As the man continued to praise Shannon, Rafe knew in his gut that Nolan Constantine was going to run for office someday. He was a very smooth operator.

Although it had taken a while for the TV crew to set up, they dismantled quickly. The radio deejay and newspaper reporters vanished. All of them were probably racing back to their desks to write up their stories to report on the conflict raised, rather than the donation. Knowing what being in the public eye was all about, Rafe realized Shannon was going to experience some fallout.

Constantine was still speaking to her on the front porch when Rafe approached them. Shannon looked distracted, as if she wasn't really hearing what her benefactor was saying.

As soon as her eyes collided with Rafe's, Constantine stopped talking. Maybe he could feel the vibrations between them. Rafe certainly could. It was as if an electric current flashed straight from Shannon's body to his.

After straightening his tie, which didn't need to be straightened, Constantine coughed.

Shannon turned to him again. "Thanks, Nolan, for trying to clean up the mess Donneker made. I don't know what's going to come of all of this—"

With his trademark smile, he patted her shoulder. "It will be fine, Shannon. We'll make it be fine. Just try to forget what happened and keep your mind on building that ring." He checked his watch. "I've got to go, but I'll be in touch. We'll go over those names of firms again who will put up the kind of building you want."

Shannon just nodded.

Finally everyone was gone. As Nolan's car sped down the gravel, Shannon turned to Rafe. "Thank you for getting Mr. Donneker to leave."

"It was the least I could do. I was just making everything worse."

In spite of all that had happened, all that had been said, she looked him squarely in the eye. "Do you believe in what I'm doing here?"

He didn't hesitate. "Yes, I do. I can't put my finger on exactly what's different with Janine, but I know something is. I know she's getting closer to you, and maybe even a little closer to me. It's in the way she looks at me and the way she takes my hand. Certainly not anything I can measure, but I do believe it's happening.''

Shannon looked relieved. ''I know you didn't believe in equine assisted therapy when you arrived, and I thought maybe your opinion hadn't changed.''

Rafe could smell Shannon's honeysuckle scent, could see the detail on the silver barrette holding back her hair. He'd love to remove it, then run his hands through her curls and kiss them away from her cheek. Restraining that urge, he concentrated on their conversation. ''The day I worked on your computer, I saw Donneker's letter in your office. Accidentally. I wasn't snooping. Why didn't you come to me for help?''

For a moment she hesitated. ''I didn't think you'd want to become involved. Besides, I'm not very good at asking for help.''

''Why is that?'' If he understood why Shannon was so independent, he'd understand *her*.

''It's a very long story.''

One she didn't tell many people, he guessed. ''I'd like to hear it sometime.''

They gazed at each other until Buster barked. The spell broken, they both turned and saw him loping toward them. Then Cora and Janine came around the side of the barn. Janine waved and came running, too, trailing after Buster.

''*That's* what's different about my daughter,'' Rafe said with a nod toward her. ''She has life in her again.''

He saw the emotion in Shannon's eyes, and he was glad he'd said it. No, Janine wasn't talking yet. Maybe that would take a very long time. But he'd seen improvement, and that was so very important.

When Cora reached the porch, she was much more

winded than Janine and gave them a rueful smile. "I'd better practice my hundred-yard dash, or she'll beat me every time. What would you folks like for supper? I have ground beef out and can make barbecue or chili or—"

"Let's go out to eat," Rafe suggested. "Into Fawn Grove. My treat."

"You don't have to do that," Shannon murmured.

"I know. But it'll give Cora a break from cooking. Besides, Janine liked their broasted chicken, didn't you, peanut?" Rafe asked, using an endearment he hadn't used in a while.

Janine's gaze stayed on his for a moment, as if she was absorbing what he'd called her, too. Then she smiled and nodded, went over a little closer to him and tucked her hand into his.

Rafe felt his chest tighten. Maybe he would get his little girl back again. And soon.

Chapter Nine

Only a few tables at the Twin Pines family restaurant were occupied as Shannon, Cora and Janine walked through the open door Rafe held for them. Early in the week, Twin Pines wasn't busy. Evening business picked up on Thursday night when beef stew was the blue plate special. Then there wasn't an empty seat in the place. The sign at the cashier's desk read Please Seat Yourself.

Rafe headed for a table back in the corner and as he did, Shannon watched Janine. The little girl looked around warily and kept close to her father. Shannon would bet Rafe hadn't taken her into many restaurants since her mother had been killed.

When Janine slipped onto the chair between Rafe and Shannon, Shannon leaned over to the little girl and put her arm around her shoulders. "Your dad said you liked the broasted chicken here. Is that true?"

Janine nodded, then pointed to an item on the back of the menu.

Shannon had to smile. She wanted a chocolate milk-shake to go with the chicken. "Sounds good to me," Shannon agreed.

When the waitress came to take their order, they all ordered broasted chicken, and Cora winked at Janine. "We're all going to have sticky fingers."

The seven-year-old smiled, then turned her attention to the placemat that had a follow-the-dots picture for children to draw and color. Shannon searched in her purse and found a red pen.

While Janine happily connected dots, Rafe's gaze locked on Shannon's. "You always seem to know what to say and do," he said.

"Not always. This afternoon was a good example."

"I think you should sue Jordy Donneker for slan-der," Cora said. Her exasperation with the man had been obvious when Shannon related what had taken place at the press conference.

"He was just making threats to scare you," Rafe insisted. "There are no guarantees in counseling or therapy. No judge would ever award him damages."

"Maybe not, but I'm worried about the harm he can do to my practice," Shannon admitted.

"You have a good reputation. That's what counts." The certainty in Rafe's green gaze emphasized his words.

Shannon hoped that was true, but it didn't take long for a rumor to damage a reputation.

The waitress brought their chicken, and although Shannon wasn't hungry, she concentrated on the meal and just enjoyed being with Cora, Rafe and Janine. She really didn't get away from the ranch much. She should probably make more of an effort. Sipping her milkshake, she glanced toward the door and recognized the redhead who'd stepped inside. As the pretty young woman looked over at the table, she spotted Shannon and came toward her. Monica Davis had covered Nolan's press conference for the *Fawn Grove Daily Register.* When Shannon had first moved to the Rocky R, Monica had written an article about her and what she'd planned for the ranch.

Without preamble the reporter dove in. "It was hectic at your ranch this afternoon, and I didn't get a chance to talk to you before I left."

Shannon introduced Monica to everyone at the table.

Afterward the reporter looked troubled. "I felt so bad about what happened today."

"How did Donneker know there would even *be* a press conference?" Rafe asked.

"I can tell you're not from Fawn Grove," Monica said with a wry smile. "Nolan Constantine made sure there was a buzz in town about his contribution to the Rocky R and the publicity he'd get from the announcement. Besides, Jordy has a sister-in-law who works in our ad department. He could have heard about it that way. I wrote up the article for tomorrow's edition, and I had to cover what Jordy said. I wish we could give you more positive press, but you know how that goes. I think the work you're doing is worthwhile."

"Maybe what you need is *more* than press coverage," Rafe suggested.

Shannon glanced over at him. "What do you mean?"

"Businesses have open houses to show the public

what they do. Why don't you have something like an open ranch day? Invite all your clients. Put a notice in the paper for anyone who's interested so they can come and look around. It might go a long way to smoothing over any doubts Donneker might have put in people's minds.''

''That's a great idea!'' Monica was enthusiastic. ''And if you have an event, I might be able to get more coverage.''

''I could answer any questions prospective clients might have...'' Shannon mused.

''If you have clients there who you've already helped, they'll add credence to your work,'' Rafe added.

Shannon thought about Rafe's suggestion as Monica left and they finished their meal.

After they drove back to the Rocky R, Janine made it known that she wanted Shannon to read her a story, and Shannon was glad to agree, eager to have something to occupy her mind other than what had happened this afternoon. One story turned into two, and then she found herself playing a board game with Rafe and his daughter. When it was Janine's bedtime, the little girl gave Shannon a hug and afterward went upstairs with Rafe.

Storing the board game on the shelf under the coffee table, Shannon knew she was too restless to settle down for the night. When she was restless, going to the barn and looking after the horses helped.

The first thing she did was to make sure Clancy had finished cleaning the stalls. He had. He was usually responsible about the chores she gave him. Working on the Rocky R seemed to be good for him.

After she fed each of the horses a carrot, she still

needed to keep her hands busy. Going to the tack room, she cleaned one of the saddles, thinking about Rafe's suggestion for good PR...thinking about Rafe.

When she'd finished, she turned off the light and headed out of the barn. The moon was full, a white medallion hanging between a few smoky clouds. Not many stars shone, but the moon was enough, lighting her way to the house. Rafe was pacing on the porch, and when he saw her he stopped.

"Is something wrong?" she asked, seeing his expression under the moonlight. The backlight from the house made him seem even more towering, more imposing, more completely male. She came up the steps slowly.

He waited until she reached the porch. "I was worried about you."

"I was in the barn."

"I figured that, but I didn't want to leave Janine alone in the house to come and find you. I was afraid you might have gone riding alone."

"This would be a perfect night for it."

They both looked up at the moon. "It wouldn't be a good idea for you to go riding alone at night. Especially if you're upset." His voice had gone lower as though he cared if she was upset.

Having someone other than Cora, especially a man, be concerned about her was a bit disconcerting. "I'm not upset. I'm just...baffled. Krissie Donneker was only in therapy for three months. Six sessions. And Jordy expected all of her problems to be solved."

"The same way I expected Janine to be able to talk in two months?"

Her gaze collided with his. "Do you still?"

"I'm hoping. But I also realize it might not happen. She might have to stay after I go back to the city."

His words were a reminder that he wouldn't be here past August fifth. She didn't want to think about that. "Thanks for your suggestion today," she murmured. "I've thought more about it, and I think it's a good idea. We could even have a barbecue to get everyone mingling and talking. I'm sure Clancy would help."

"Probably the sooner you have it, the better."

"It shouldn't be too hard to arrange. I can call an ad into the paper tomorrow."

"For when?" Rafe asked.

"Two weeks from Sunday."

There was a bond growing between her and Rafe, whether they wanted it or not. Afraid to call it by anything else, afraid of what it could mean to her heart, let alone her life, she decided, "I'd better go in."

Before she could, Rafe caught her hand. "Shannon?"

She raised her gaze to his. "Yes?"

"I might not have believed in your work when I first arrived. But I've seen you, not just with Janine but with the other kids, too. I've seen how they've gained confidence. I've seen how they've learned how to balance their lives, not just their physical bodies while they're riding...how each of them has learned to take control yet work as a partner with their horse. All of that teaches so much more than words ever could."

Rafe's belief in her work made her throat constrict. "Thank you for saying that."

He brought her hand to his lips, kissing the palm

and rubbing his thumb over the soft skin there. "You're a special woman, Shannon Collins."

The touch of his lips on her skin, his finger caressing her, made her insides melt as his praise flowed over her. It was something she needed to hear... something she'd needed to hear all her life. She saw the sparks of desire in his eyes, saw the wanting and wished she could give in to the moment. But she couldn't. She'd trained herself not to be reckless, to take measured steps to reach a specific goal.

In the face of the passion they could share, goals didn't seem very important. Yet she knew she wanted more than Rafe was offering. She wanted more than a few weeks of pleasure.

Before they got entangled in an embrace or a kiss that she might not be able to halt, she quickly raised herself on tiptoe and kissed his cheek. Then she pulled her hand from his and went into the house, feeling as if she'd left a part of her outside, feeling as if her bond with Rafe was more important than any bond she'd ever had.

Instead of working on the pavilion while Janine was in therapy the next morning, Rafe went for a jog. Tonight after supper while Janine stayed with Cora or Shannon, he would have a couple of hours to shingle the roof. The structure was looking good, and he felt productive in a way he hadn't in years. Maybe the inside of a courtroom and the paperwork on his desk should be a thing of the past.

In the first half of his run he concentrated on his breathing, letting the exertion sweep away all thought. When he made his return trip and sweat ran down his temples and along his cheek, he remembered Shannon's kiss on the porch last night. It had been such a simple meeting of her lips against his skin, but he'd continued to feel it all night. As he'd looked in the mirror this morning, he'd felt as if an indelible mark should be there.

Slowing as the barn came into sight, he spotted Janine and Shannon in the corral with Marigold, golden sunlight shining on them. Janine was riding bareback, a riding helmet on her head, and she looked as pleased as punch, as if she were sitting on top of the world. Shannon led the pony slowly around the corral while Janine held on to Marigold's mane. Rafe stood there watching his daughter try something exciting and new. There was no hint of fear in her demeanor, and he realized that was because she was intent on balancing herself on the animal while she enjoyed the ride.

When Shannon brought Marigold to a stop, she helped his daughter dismount. Then she said something to Janine, and the little girl scurried into the barn.

Rafe approached the corral gate at the same time Cora emerged from Shannon's office, frowning, with a slip of paper in her hand. When she reached Shannon, she looked troubled.

Shannon met them both at the gate. "What is it, Aunt Cora?"

"Your two afternoon appointments canceled," her aunt said.

"What? What reason did they give?"

"Mrs. Caraway mumbled an excuse about not feeling well."

"How do you know it was an excuse?"

"I could tell by her voice she wasn't telling the truth. When I asked her when she wanted to reschedule, she said she didn't know what next week would bring and she'd have to call you. Hogwash! At least Joan Felton was honest when she called. She said she saw the bit on the news last night about you and the Rocky R. She wants to rethink the idea of equine therapy for her son. She said she'll be in touch when she decides whether she'll continue with it or look for a more traditional therapist.''

Rafe could see that Shannon was upset and trying to hide it. ''You knew there would be repercussions,'' he reminded her gently.

''I guess I was hoping there wouldn't be.'' She sighed. ''I'm not sure *what* I was hoping.''

He moved closer to the gate. ''Did you put the ad in the paper yet?''

''No. But it looks as if I'll have all afternoon to do it.''

Janine came running from the barn, grooming brush in hand. He'd intended to take her to a park in Sacramento this afternoon where there were paddle boats and a puppet show. Now he decided the outing would do Shannon some good, as well as him and his daughter. ''Janine and I were going to drive into Sacramento this afternoon and spend some time in the park. Why don't you come along with us?''

''I have paperwork I can catch up on...and chores.''

He wondered if Shannon truly had work to do, or if she was just trying to keep her distance. ''A little fun wouldn't hurt. We could discuss specifically what you want to do for the open ranch day.''

Janine was happily running the brush over Marigold's neck when Shannon glanced at her and then back at him. ''Maybe Janine would rather spend the time alone with you.''

"She's had nothing *but* time alone with me. I'm sure she'd welcome your company."

Cora put her two cents in. "Don't worry about anything here. I'll mind the fort. It would do you good to go into the city. You can even pack a picnic and have a late lunch."

"It sounds good to me." Rafe's gaze locked to Shannon's.

"It sounds good to me, too," she finally said with a smile. "It'll keep me from fretting over losing clients. Just give me fifteen minutes to change and I'll be ready."

When Shannon disembarked from the paddleboat an attendant was holding steady, she saw Janine tug on Rafe's elbow and point to the playground about fifty feet away.

He looked up at the sky, where gray had overtaken blue and clouds skittered with the breeze. "For a little while," he said. "It looks like it might storm."

Janine just shrugged and ran ahead of him toward the playground with its sliding boards and jungle gym, monkey bars and swings.

Shannon fell into step beside him as they followed his daughter. "I think she's going to wear us out!"

He chuckled. "It's so good to see her active again. She used to be like this all the time, but then it was as if a light shut off inside of her."

"That's changing now."

Rafe gave Shannon a look that was filled with gratitude, but a lot more too, and she felt her heart speed up. They'd had a lovely afternoon, picnicking under an oak, feeding ducks by the pond, crossing the lake in paddle boats. It was almost as if they were a family.

But they weren't. Still, she felt the bonds tightening among them. Even Rafe seemed almost relaxed today, except when their skin had inadvertently touched, when their eyes had met or when Janine wandered a little too far away to be a good chaperone. Now with his daughter heading toward the jungle gym, Rafe guided Shannon to a bench near a row of oaks. The wind was picking up and blew her hair across her cheek.

At that moment Rafe turned to look at her, and before she could anticipate the gesture, he reached out and his thumb pushed her hair away from her face. The tingles that began on her cheek invaded her whole body, and she felt herself flush. "I've had a really good time today."

"Me, too. I'd forgotten what having fun meant. I'd forgotten how being with someone makes everything twice as enjoyable." He leaned a bit closer. "Being with you does that."

"You sound surprised."

"I guess I am. When Nancy and I would take Janine out, it was usually to the movies or to a toy store. Nancy wasn't an outdoor person."

Shannon had wondered often about Rafe's wife and what she was like. "Does Janine look like her?" Shannon asked.

"She has my hair and eyes, but Nancy's face, for sure. Nancy was a beautiful woman."

Shannon's heart sank a little. She'd never be considered beautiful. Attractive, maybe. "Did Nancy work?"

"No. She always said her full-time job was taking care of Janine and the house. She did it beautifully, too. It was just—"

"What?"

He looked troubled. "Nothing."

They sat in silence a few moments until Rafe eventually continued in a low voice, "She needed me so much, Shannon. She was that kind of woman. She depended on me for her happiness, her safety, her life."

"Marriage is about two people needing each other."

"I never want anyone to need me that way again."

As thunder grumbled and the sky grew darker, Shannon realized her joy in the day had dimmed with the talk of Rafe's wife. Rafe was a strong, forceful man and she could understand how easy it would be to depend on him. To need him. To love him. Like the bolt of lightning that suddenly streaked across the sky, she knew what she was feeling was love. She loved Rafe Pierson, and she loved his daughter. Her life wouldn't be the same when they left.

At the first crack of thunder, Janine came running toward them, looking anxious.

As huge drops plopped on them, children and parents and sight-seers scattered for cover. Janine's eyes darted here and there, and Shannon wondered if the chaos reminded her of that day in the restaurant.

Rafe took his daughter's hand. "Let's run to the parking lot. The car will be the safest place."

Suddenly the clouds opened and rain poured down. Rafe scooped up Janine into his arms, and as thunder grumbled again and lightning shot through the sky, she had her hands over her ears as if to block out the sounds reminiscent of gunfire.

Shannon kept up with Rafe's long-legged jog somehow. He kept glancing at her to make sure he wasn't leaving her behind. When they reached the parking lot, he fumbled in his jeans pocket for his key and the remote. Shannon heard the beep and the click as they approached his car, signaling the doors were unlocked.

Janine's arms were tight around her dad's neck, and she was clinging to him. When he opened the passenger door and tried to put Janine inside, she wouldn't let go, although they were all getting soaked.

Shannon bent close to Janine and murmured to her, "Come on. Let's get into the car so we don't get any more wet than we already are."

Janine held her arms out to Shannon, and Shannon took her into the passenger's seat, holding her close, while Rafe raced around to the driver's side and slid in.

The little girl huddled against Shannon, seeking more than warmth.

Turning to his daughter, Rafe stroked down the top of her head. "It's okay, baby. It's just thunder. We got a little wet, but we'll dry off."

When the thunder cracked again, Janine stayed huddled against Shannon. This time Shannon stroked the seven-year-old's hair. "Let's talk about something else. I'm thinking about planning a party so lots of kids and their parents can get to know the horses better and look around the ranch. I thought maybe I'd have Clancy give them rides on Marigold. What do you think?"

Rafe sat looking on as eventually his daughter stopped trembling and raised her gaze to Shannon's. He'd been afraid the chaos and the storm would send Janine back to her inner world again. Now as he saw color returning to her cheeks, and the nods and shakes of her head as Shannon spoke to her and questioned her, she seemed to be responding. She seemed to be okay.

He sent up a grateful prayer and realized it was the first time he'd prayed since his world had come crashing down on him. Even in church with Shannon, he hadn't been able to. But now...

He was afraid he was becoming as attached to Shannon as his daughter was! His desire for her was steadily becoming harder to handle and terrifically unsettled him. Worse still, he cared about her. A fling for a few weeks to help him forget was one thing, getting involved was another. Yet he wanted to be with Shannon. Somehow she soothed the anger that had lived inside of him over the past months, and she even led him to hope that life could be good again.

Switching on the ignition, he flipped the heat control to dispel the damp chill.

Seeing Janine was fully involved in the idea of a day at the ranch with a barbecue and games, he started the windshield wipers.

Then he patted the seat in the middle. "How about sitting over here?" he asked his daughter. "We'll find the nearest store and get a few towels."

Janine didn't avoid his gaze but scrambled between the two adults, looking calm again, looking as if sitting between him and Shannon was exactly where she wanted to be.

Following Shannon's directions, Rafe drove to the nearest store. He insisted he'd go inside and get what they needed. There was no point in all three of them getting chilled in the air-conditioning.

Fifteen minutes later he returned with three blue towels, new shorts with a top for Janine, and dry T-shirts for him and Shannon. He simply said, "It'll make the drive home more comfortable.'' Then he drove to a gas station with a convenience store and bathrooms where they changed into their new duds, bought coffee for him and Shannon and hot chocolate for Janine. During the drive back to the ranch, as the brief storm blew over, his daughter fell asleep in the back seat.

When they arrived at the Rocky R, Cora was waiting for them. ''I was worried you folks might have gotten drenched.'' Her gaze passed over Shannon and Rafe's still-wet jeans, their wet hair, although his was mostly dry now. She put her arm around Janine's shoulders. ''Why don't we go upstairs and dry your hair? Then we'll talk about what you want for supper.''

Rafe realized Janine didn't hesitate to go with Cora. Life here had become second nature to her, and he knew it had become second nature to him, too.

When Shannon ran her hand through her hair, he noticed how big the T-shirt was on her. It hung halfway down her thighs over her jeans.

''I think I'll get changed, too. Not that I don't love my new Dodgers shirt,'' she joked.

''I just grabbed something,'' he said with a grin. ''But you could wear that as a dress and get away with it.''

She laughed. ''Hardly. A nightshirt maybe.''

Visions of her in her nightshirt brought back the memory of kissing her and touching her in his bed. She must have remembered, too, because her face flushed.

''You really helped Janine this afternoon.'' He couldn't keep the huskiness from his voice.

"I'll try to work her through what happened today in our session tomorrow."

"Has she drawn any pictures of Nancy or the restaurant?"

"She won't even let me get close to the subject. She turns me off. Just won't answer, or wants to leave the office. I don't want to make an issue of all of it until she's ready to deal with it. I lead her and hope she'll follow."

"Where do you get your patience?" he asked.

"I guess I've always been a patient person," she responded with a smile.

"And I *never* have been."

"You're kidding," she teased with good-natured wryness.

"Watch it, or the next time I'll buy you a T-shirt that's too small," he growled.

She laughed. But when her gaze met his, the smile slipped away. He knew they were both remembering the night he'd pushed up her nightshirt to caress her. There was an ache inside Rafe that began with desire but ended someplace altogether different. Only Shannon seemed to ease it. Kissing and touching her was the beginning. Physical satisfaction should be the end of it. Maybe he needed to find out. Maybe if he got enough of Shannon, the rest of it would go away.

"How long has it been since you went out for a night on the town?"

She looked surprised. "Just what *is* a night on the town?"

"Dinner. Dancing. Not getting home until at least after midnight."

"I haven't had a night like that in a very long time."

"Then you're due. I saw an ad in the paper for a new restaurant on this side of Sacramento. The Top Hat Inn. They have a band every weekend. How about Saturday night you and I go dining and dancing?"

For a few moments, he thought she was going to refuse. Then the look in her eyes told him she wanted to be alone with him, as much as he wanted to be alone with her. Away from the Rocky R. Away from his daughter. Away from his past.

"I'd like that." Her voice was low, as if she was admitting it to herself as well as to him.

Closing the small gap between them, he slid his hands into her wet hair, tilted her chin up and kissed her full on the lips. It was quick and hot, and he'd wanted to do it all day. When he raised his head and saw her startled look, he murmured, "It must be that T-shirt. It makes you irresistible." Then he grinned at her and realized he felt almost happy for the first time in months.

Her color high, she backed away from him. "Then I guess I'd better be careful when I wear it."

At that she turned and fled to her room.

Rafe liked the idea of rattling Shannon Collins. He liked her cheeks going rosy. He liked seeing her lips pink after he'd kissed her. They were going to have one hell of a good time Saturday night if he had anything to say about it.

After dining and dancing he might even rent a room at the inn.

Chapter Ten

Rafe laid his navy suitcoat over the back of a living room chair and watched Cora and Janine play a game of crazy eights as he waited for Shannon. From Janine's side, Buster glanced up at Rafe as if he didn't know him in the dress clothes.

Rafe was about to go out onto the porch to wait, hoping to pick up a cool breeze, when Shannon came into the living room from the hall leading to her bedroom. The sight of her hit him like an arrow finding its mark in a bull's-eye. He knew she had curves any woman would envy, coupled with a slenderness that made her look good even in jeans and T-shirt. Tonight, though, she looked like a different woman from the one who spoke softly to horses, as well as to his daughter. She was wearing a black linen dress trimmed in white. It had short, puffed sleeves, a square neck that showed off her creamy skin, and a slim skirt trimmed with white at the hem that came just to her knees. With her patent-leather high heels, her legs looked long, and he felt his body already tightening with anticipation of feeling her against him. She'd swept her hair up into a topknot, and curls fell everywhere. They tempted and teased around her face, begging to be touched. Her earrings were black onyx trimmed in gold, and a matching oval necklace lay delicately at her throat. She was absolutely stunning.

Over her arm she carried a silky white shawl with long fringes. She lifted it slightly. "I thought I'd take this along in case the restaurant's cool."

Before he thought better of it he responded, "I'll keep you warm." He knew his hunger for her had to show in his eyes. But tonight he didn't care. Tonight they'd live moment by moment and let the evening take them to a natural conclusion. He was hoping Shannon would want the same conclusion he did.

Cora cleared her throat loudly, and Rafe realized he and Shannon had been standing there for several long moments, just gazing at each other.

"I have Rafe's cell phone number," Cora reminded them. "But I don't expect I'll have to use it. Janine and I are going to play cards until I win a game, then watch TV and have hot-fudge sundaes. So don't you worry about us."

Rafe had been concerned about leaving Janine tonight, but he'd talked to her about it and she'd seemed unconcerned that he and Shannon were going out for dinner and wouldn't be back until late. She'd just motioned to her stack of books, games, Cora and Buster, and given him a small smile and a shrug that told him she should be fine.

He was beginning to believe she might be.

Tonight he didn't want to think about anything but Shannon—and now—and how the night could end.

"Are you ready?" he asked.

"Yes." There was a decisiveness in Shannon's answer, and a sense of promise. She might be a dreamer, but she knew about trade-offs, too. Capturing all they could for as long as they could might satisfy them both.

They drove through Fawn Grove, then took the highway leading to Sacramento. Shannon had been quiet since they'd left the ranch, and he wondered what she was thinking. "Have you had any more cancellations?"

When she glanced over at him, her expression was serious. "Two more. I'm hoping if clients haven't called by now, they won't. It's prospective clients that I'm concerned about."

"Having the Rocky R open to the public will solve that."

"You seem so sure."

"All they have to do is talk with you and see how you relate to the kids and the horses. If it takes more than that, then you probably don't want to work with them."

She smiled at his logic. "I hope you're right."

Her hands were lying in her lap, and he reached over and covered one of them with his. "I know I'm right. And now, for the rest of tonight, you can't think about the Rocky R or your work. Got it?"

"What am I supposed to think about?" she asked flippantly.

"A man and a woman having a very good time." He knew the huskiness of his voice conveyed exactly what he wanted to do with her. He sensed her sharp intake of breath, as if she was imagining having that very good time.

Rubbing his thumb sensually across hers, he added, "Tonight is just for us."

Shannon didn't respond. She didn't protest or ask what he meant, either, because they both knew the sparks between them from the first day they'd met had been fueled by tastes and touches of desire. He suspected she couldn't deny the need and hunger growing between them any more than he could.

The Top Hat Inn had a classy restaurant with the look of another era. The building housing the restaurant was a stately brick that looked more like a mansion than an inn. Though the parking lot was large, it was three-quarters filled. Rafe found a spot, expertly pulled in and switched off the ignition.

When he glanced over at Shannon, he could feel a terrific pull toward her. His body was already revved up because of the sweet scent of her, the creamy length of her arms so close to his, her smile that was almost shy when she glanced at him. He'd never considered Shannon shy, but maybe she felt the same anticipatory excitement that he did.

Unfastening his seat belt, he climbed out of the car and went around to her door. When he opened it, he offered her his hand and she took it. After he'd assisted her out, he didn't let go but tugged her close to his chest.

She gazed up at him with wide, brown eyes that seemed entirely too innocent and vulnerable. Instead of kissing her on the mouth, he brushed his lips across her temple, murmuring, "This is going to be a night to remember."

Shannon trembled when Rafe's lips brushed her

skin. She knew this *could* be a night to remember if she let it. She loved Rafe Pierson. Could she forget about the future and dreams and grab on to what she could have now? Wouldn't that be more than she'd *ever* had?

Twining her arms around Rafe's neck, she kissed him lightly on the mouth. ''Then let's get started.''

His emerald-green eyes now held a fire that she wanted to experience. When, where and how didn't seem to matter much. They'd just take the night one special moment by one special moment.

Rafe tucked her hand into the crook of his arm, and they walked up the brick path to the front door where wrought-iron gas lights burned on either side, like beacons in the onset of dusk. Inside, they found a hostess dressed in a red chiffon gown reminiscent of the Big Band Era. There were pictures of Tommy Dorsey and Guy Lombardo, Cyd Charisse and Fred Astaire on the walls, along with a three-foot poster advertising *Singing in the Rain.*

As the hostess showed Shannon and Rafe to their table, Shannon noticed that the waiters were dressed in tails and the large room was decorated in black and silver. There were small vases on each table resembling top hats, containing white carnations and ferns. Small candles in crystal globes flickered where patrons were seated. Some of the smaller tables, with their white tablecloths, were fairly close together. There was a quietness about the room, even with the low voices, that said diners came here to spend a private evening with someone special, eating excellent cuisine and savoring the good things in life.

Before the waiter seated her, Shannon glimpsed a grand piano at one corner of the dance floor and the setup for a band. The waiter lit their candle, handed Rafe the wine list and departed.

Rafe laid the small leather folder on the table and eyed Shannon over the candle. "What do you think?"

"I think this place is wonderful."

He tapped the wine list. "I think it's only fitting we have champagne, don't you?"

She felt a bit embarrassed, but wanted Rafe to know just how many new experiences he was leading her into. "I've never had champagne."

His brows arched. "You're kidding."

Giving a little shrug, she explained, "I guess the right occasion never came up."

"What about your engagement?"

"That was pretty cut-and-dried. Allen brought over a bottle of Chianti and we had it with pizza."

Rafe's brow creased, and he shook his head. "Chianti and pizza are great. But champagne and lobster are even better. You *have* eaten lobster?" he asked with a slow, crooked grin.

"Yes, I have. And I love it."

They found so many subjects to talk about as they sipped champagne and waited for their orders. Every once and a while their gazes would collide, and one of them would lose their train of thought. Then she or Rafe would smile, and they'd move onto something else.

A couple who looked to be in their midtwenties was seated at the table next to them. Shannon glanced at them briefly and saw that the young brunette wasn't smiling. The young man with her looked much more relaxed. Their tables were close enough that as she and Rafe talked, she heard the man order for both of them. The woman started to protest, but the man gave her a sharp look, and she was instantly quiet. Shannon told herself she was reading too much into the interchange and turned her attention back to the succulent lobster the waiter placed in front of her and the intense fire in Rafe's green eyes.

The band began playing, first dinner music and then old-fashioned melodies that Shannon recognized because her mother had tuned in often to a radio station that played them. "Twilight Time" wrapped around their table as Shannon and Rafe ate their dinner with a growing sensual awareness between them. Once, he reached over and brushed a lingering spot of melted butter from the corner of her lip. He did it easily, slowly, looking into her eyes, watching her response.

She felt as if everything between them was almost magical tonight. His knee grazed hers under the table, and she didn't move away. Her whole body tingled. Her champagne glass was empty now, but she still felt as if golden bubbles were dancing excitedly inside of her. The chocolate cheesecake they ordered for dessert was as temptingly wicked as the depths of Rafe's green eyes. They followed it with demitasse cups of espresso.

When the band began the strains of "Fascination," Rafe stood and held out his hand to Shannon. She took it and followed him to the dance floor. Gathering her into a ballroom position, he swept her onto the floor, expertly guiding her. He was easy to follow, easy to hold on to, easy to want in a way she'd never wanted a man. He was devastatingly handsome tonight in his navy suit, white dress shirt, and red-and-navy silk tie. She didn't once trip or miss a step, and the music flowed smoothly, making her almost dizzy.

After the next melody began, she noticed it was

much slower and she didn't recognize it. Rafe drew her closer into his arms, brought their hands into his chest, and held her possessively. The sheer romantic thrill of the night, and the music, and being held in Rafe's arms was intoxicating. His hand was making caressing circles on her back, and she knew he could feel her trembling.

"Shannon?" he asked. His face was so very close to hers.

"What?" she breathed.

"You're the most beautiful woman here tonight."

She wasn't the type of woman men used lines on, but she could tell this was no line. Rafe meant it, and she felt herself melting deeper into him. "No one's ever called me beautiful before."

"Then they're all fools."

The heat generated by their bodies pressed together almost made Shannon feel wild...wanton...driven. The anticipation of being wrapped in Rafe's arms, being one with him, thrilled her in ways she never expected, making her insides feel like hot lava, urging her to think in the moment, feel in the moment and forget about the future.

Slowly he lowered his head. His lips sealed to hers, and she thought about nothing but now. Although there were couples dancing around them, Shannon was unmindful of anything except Rafe—the hot wetness of his tongue, the lingering taste of chocolate and expresso, the excitement and arousal that were so new to her. Allen's kisses and lovemaking had been competent, but never fiery, never all-consuming, never possessively demanding. She'd thought that was what she'd wanted. She'd been wrong.

When Rafe broke the kiss and raised his head, his breathing was ragged and she understood why.

"We'd better slow this down." His voice was husky as he put a little space between them. "Let's go back to the table."

He kept his arm around Shannon as they made their way through the dancers. After he pulled out a chair and seated her, he took his chair across from her.

The music stopped, and Shannon was aware that the couple at the table closest to them seemed to be having a heated conversation. She tried to block it out, and as Rafe's gaze settled on her face, she did.

Reaching across the table, he took her hand and intertwined his fingers with hers. "How would you feel about getting a room so we can go some place private?"

She knew exactly what he was asking her, and she knew she wanted the intimacy Rafe was offering. When she opened her mouth to tell him she liked his idea, the words never came out.

At the table next to them, the man jumped to his feet and angrily grabbed the woman's arm. "I said we're going to dance."

"Not when you've been drinking," the brunette pleaded. "And you can't drive home like this, either."

Angrily he yanked her to her feet. "Don't you tell me what I am and am not going to do. *You* take orders from *me*."

The woman's voice shook when she spoke, and she looked scared. "Not this time." She turned and walked out.

The man's furious words, the expression on his face, seemed to toss Shannon back in time. She could hear another man's voice—her father's. She could see her mother's face. She could hear her mother moan…

"What's wrong, Shannon?"

Although she realized she was still holding Rafe's hand, her fingertips felt numb. "I…nothing's wrong."

"The hell it isn't. You're white."

She felt hot and cold and needed fresh air to take deep breaths to clear her body and her mind of memories that had been buried for a very long time.

Standing, Rafe came around to her and pulled her out of her chair. Then he picked up her purse, handed it to her and draped her shawl around her shoulders. "Come on. Let's go outside for a few minutes."

Shannon let Rafe guide her through the restaurant, through the foyer and outside. A car sped past them, and Shannon spotted the driver—the brunette from the table next to theirs. Maybe tonight she was leaving her husband. Maybe she wouldn't wait to sneak away in the dead of night.

Rafe's arm was protective around Shannon. Ever since he'd come into her life, feelings she'd forgotten had bubbled up. Her emotions seemed more intense. Had she been frozen all these years to protect herself from falling in love? Why was her love for Rafe and for his daughter reopening her old wounds?

Because maybe they never healed, a small voice whispered. *You willed it behind you but maybe it never really* was *behind you.*

Instead of guiding her toward the parking lot, Rafe turned in the other direction toward a walk of flagstones that wound through a grove of pines. He stopped just beyond the pool of lights beaming from the front of the restaurant. "Tell me what happened in there," he demanded gently.

Old habits took over. "It was nothing, Rafe. Really. I just…" Her voice wavered, and she realized if she wanted him to know her—really know her—she had to tell him what had upset her. "That scene inside triggered a flash from the past."

"Did your fiancé abuse you?" he asked gruffly.

"No. But my father abused my mother. It went on until I was nine. He didn't need alcohol to make him mean. There was no logic to it. My mother tried to give him everything he wanted, please him in every way, make their life perfect. She couldn't. He'd never tell her exactly when he'd be home for supper, but if dinner wasn't ready when he came home, he'd slap her. Or worse."

"And you saw all of this?"

"I spent a lot of time in my room when my father was there, where I'd be out of his way. I wondered if the fighting was my fault…if somehow *I* was the one who was doing something wrong."

"But you learned differently, I hope."

"Eventually. After we got out."

"Your mother finally left him?"

This was the hard part, the part she'd once confided in a mentor but never to anyone else. "One night he was particularly angry about something that happened at work. Mom served something he didn't like or want. He threw it on the floor and then he went after her. I'd always stayed out of it before, like mom wanted. But I couldn't stand to watch him hit her again. So I got between them."

She shivered thinking about it. "He grabbed me instead of Mom…so hard that he dislocated my shoulder. Then he backhanded me. Somehow my mother grabbed me and rushed me into her bedroom, locking the door. He pounded on it. I thought the wood would break and he'd come in, anyway. But after he kicked it, he left the apartment. My mother threw a few things into a suitcase, grabbed the money she'd saved and took me to the emergency room. A nurse there helped find a shelter for us. We were living in San Francisco then, but Aunt Cora was in Sacramento. After a few nights in the shelter my mother phoned Aunt Cora and we went to live with her until we got our own apartment and my mom found a job. Neither of us really felt safe until a year later when we learned my father had been killed in a brawl.''

Rafe wrapped his arms around her. ''You're trembling.''

She was. And she couldn't understand it. She'd forgotten about all of it. She'd put it all in the past. But now it was there—in her heart and in her head, as if she were a child again.

Rafe held her for long, silent moments. Then his voice was raspy when he spoke. ''I'm sorry you had to go through that.'' Resting his chin on top of her hair, he stroked her back, soothing her, calming her.

Finally she looked up at him. ''I don't know why all of this is coming back now.'' She felt so very vulnerable. Is that what love did?

Inside, a few minutes ago, she'd been about to accept Rafe's invitation to take a room for the night…to make love with him. If she made love with Rafe Pierson, she'd lose her heart completely. She'd be giving him unequivocal power over her. The risk might be worth it…if she knew she had the same kind of power over him. But she didn't. Rafe desired her, but she didn't know how much he cared about her. Just as she'd guarded her heart all these years, he was guarding his now. He was determined not to get involved. He wanted physical pleasure, not commitment and promises, and a future together. It hit Shannon hard that she could see so clearly that *she* yearned for commitment and promises and a life together with Rafe.

He'd said his wife had needed him too much and he never wanted anyone to need him that way again. Shannon didn't want to need him, but she did. It was a need she'd have to deny if she wanted to remain whole, if she wanted to remain in control of her own life, if she wanted to *not* fall apart when Rafe left.

Leaning away from him, she murmured, "I think we'd better go back to the ranch."

His expression was sober when he looked down at her. "All right. If that's what you want."

"That's what I want."

Rafe dropped his arms to his sides, and she felt bereft without them around her. All evening they had seemed so close, and now there was distance again between them.

But she knew distance was safer for both of them.

After church service on Sunday, Shannon turned the horses into the pasture, thinking about her silent ride home from Sacramento with Rafe the night before. After they'd returned to the Rocky R, they'd said good-night. Rafe hadn't kissed her or touched her. She'd asked to come home instead of staying in a room at the inn with him. He wasn't the type of man to push...or to ask twice.

Shannon closed the gate to the pasture and walked around Marigold's shed. When she heard a soft mumbling, she stopped and carefully peeked around the smaller structure. Janine was feeding the pony an apple, whispering to her. Shannon couldn't hear what the little girl was saying, but the point was—she was talking.

If she told Rafe...

He might try to force Janine to talk sooner than she was ready to.

The crunch of tires on gravel alerted Shannon to a car coming down the lane. Janine's whispering stopped. Shannon kicked gravel coming around the corner of the shed so Janine would know she was there. "It looks like we have visitors, honey. Let's go up to the house."

Janine tucked her hand into Shannon's and walked beside her as they rounded the grassy side of the barn and crossed to the porch. Cora was standing there talking to a man who was about five-eight with medium-brown hair. He wore a white polo shirt with casual trousers, and Shannon wondered who he was.

But when Rafe came outside, it was obvious he knew the man. "Sam. What are you doing here?"

Sam looked Rafe up and down, from his faded T-shirt and jeans to his black boots. "Don't you look like you're on vacation!"

"I guess you know this fellow?" Cora asked with a smile.

Shannon and Janine had come up onto the porch by then, and Rafe introduced their guest. "Sam Patterson, this is Shannon Collins, the owner of the Rocky R. You know Janine. And this is Shannon's Aunt Cora. Sam's a deputy D.A. and works with me back in Salinas."

After Sam nodded to Shannon, he addressed Rafe again. "Duncan sent me to find out when you'd be back. He never expected you to be gone this long."

"I took a leave for two months."

"Yeah. Well, I'm supposed to convince you to come back sooner. Duncan says he's invested too much time and effort into you to let you stray for any length of time."

The two men stared at each other in silent communication until Rafe repeated, "I took two months, and I'll be away for two months."

Cora broke the tension. "Would you like to stay for lunch, Mr. Patterson? We were just about to sit down."

With a conciliatory smile, Sam nodded. "I'd like that. Maybe I can talk some sense into the man who's supposed to be the next D.A. of Monterey County."

Rafe's gaze connected with Shannon's, and her heart gave a lurch. Rafe might be rethinking his career, but he wouldn't give up the opportunity to move into a position as prestigious as district attorney. Any hopes she had about him staying, any dreams she might have nurtured, were as intangible as wisps of smoke in a breeze.

Rafe Pierson had a life in Salinas, and he would be returning to it.

Chapter Eleven

After Rafe put Janine to bed on Sunday night, he felt restless and frustrated and altogether out of sorts. The evening with Shannon last night had been a revelation, not only of her background but of how much he wanted her. When she'd told him about her childhood, he'd realized why she'd become a psychologist, why she was so dedicated to helping children overcome their fears. He understood her so much better now— her need for independence, her need to feel free.

Yet he'd been bitterly disappointed when she'd asked him to take her home. He had seen the remnants of memories in her eyes and had wanted to kiss them and pleasure them away. But apparently what had happened last night had made her feel much too vulnerable to even think about being intimate with a man.

When he descended the stairs, Cora was sitting in the living room watching TV. While Shannon had mumbled something about paperwork after supper and had vanished into her office, Cora had stayed at the house, sitting on the swing on the porch with Janine, teaching her how to do cross-stitch. Now she looked up at him from the sofa with one of those know-it-all smiles. "She's in the barn, if you're lookin'."

Was he looking? Just how much further did he want to go with Shannon? "I don't want to leave Janine alone in the house."

"She won't be alone. I'll stay until you or Shannon come back."

He supposed they *should* clear the air. He supposed they should finish whatever they'd started last night, no matter how it went. "I won't be long," he said, as he went to the door.

"Take your time. This old movie has me hooked."

The night was starless, and only a shadow of a moon glowed beyond the film of clouds. Rafe crossed the front yard and then the gravel lane, mulling over Sam Patterson's visit. That had come as a surprise, along with the message that if he wanted the D.A.'s position when Duncan Forsythe retired, he'd better get his tail back to Salinas.

He'd never handled ultimatums very well.

Opening the corral gate, Rafe saw that the barn door was ajar. What was Shannon doing out here so late?

The answer to that question came fast. *Staying away from you.*

When he went inside, he saw her standing at the end of the row by Gray Lady's stall, murmuring to the horse. A grooming brush sat on the top rung of the gate. An overhead bulb in the walkway between stalls enabled Rafe to see the troubled expression on Shannon's face as she spotted him.

"Avoiding me isn't going to solve any of your problems."

Her chin came up, and her brown eyes flashed the independence he'd seen there so many times before. "I don't have any problems."

"The hell you don't. You want me as much as I want you, but you're fighting it for all you're worth."

There was an empty stall between Gray Lady and Cloppy. A pile of blankets were stacked on one of the hay bales there. Shannon turned away from him and went toward them. "I don't want to discuss this. You're going back to Salinas soon, and none of what we're feeling is going to matter."

Her dismissal of him and the desire that had gripped him so strongly ever since he'd arrived urged him to move toward her quickly...to clasp her arm...to spin her around. "Don't tell me this doesn't matter."

Ignoring her small gasp of surprise, he enfolded her in his arms and sealed his lips to hers. For an aching eternity it seemed, he just kept his lips pressed to hers, telling her he wouldn't force her into anything, yet coaxing her not to deny the desire between them. His knowledge of Shannon, as well as his instincts, forced him to wait patiently, to hold on to his control, to restrain the arousal that demanded to be satisfied. He ached from wanting her and needing her.

While he waited, Shannon's stubbornness and her determination to keep distance between them began to melt away. He felt her become less rigid in his arms. Taking that as a sign, he brushed his lips back and forth across hers and nibbled at the corner of her lip. With a small moan, she put her arms around his neck and threaded her fingers into his hair. He knew then she couldn't resist the powerful force between them any more than he could. One of her hands lowered to the nape of his neck, and she stroked there.

When he could no longer stand the sensual pleasure of it, he slipped his tongue into her mouth. Each glide of his tongue brought a response from her until she was as involved as he was…until the heat between them became steam…until the earth fell away, leaving the two of them to hold on to each other. Something about this kiss was different from any other they'd shared. Something about this kiss told him she wanted the same pleasure he did.

When Shannon gave in to the seduction of Rafe's kiss, she knew full well what she was doing. She'd done nothing but think about making love with him since last night. She'd been telling herself she couldn't be with Rafe because he was going to leave. Because he didn't believe in commitment. Because he never wanted to marry again. Nothing had changed any of that. But *she* had changed with loving him. What if tonight was the only night they'd have? What if tonight she could *truly* understand what it meant to be known by a man? Why should she deprive herself of part of a dream she might never know again?

All the questions, all the thoughts, swirled into the night as Rafe's hands went to the buttons on her blouse and he began to unfasten them.

She wanted to touch his skin. She wanted to have the freedom to swirl her fingers through his chest hair and know every muscled inch of him. Maybe after they made love he'd realize what they could have. Maybe his love for her would grow, as hers had for him.

They were hardly aware of where their boots and clothes landed. They couldn't keep their hands off each other. Or their lips. With the scent of hay and the intoxicating musk of Rafe's skin surrounding her, Shannon let Rafe take her down on top of their clothes in the vacant stall. He kissed her so deeply she could hardly remember when he wasn't kissing her. His body was long and muscled and strong, and she passed her hands over as much of it as she could.

When he spread her legs she welcomed him—all of him—in a mind-boggling burst of pleasure that she would never, ever forget. Sensation built upon sensation as he moved inside of her—hot, and hard and powerful. She'd never known a climax before, and as one wave of pleasure crashed into the next, she drew Rafe deeper and deeper inside of her, praying for their union to never end, holding on to each shining moment of it with her heart and her hands and everything she was. Her climax was so shattering, she cried Rafe's name over and over again. Seconds later he called hers. As the world spun, she held on to him, knowing she'd found something tonight she'd never expected to find. She'd always had an emptiness inside of her. Tonight that emptiness had been filled. Tonight, she felt whole.

Shannon was still catching her breath when Rafe rolled off her and lay on his side. She reached up to stroke his face, but when she saw his expression, her hand stilled. ''What is it?''

His voice was gruff. ''Last night I was prepared for this. Tonight I wasn't. Are you by any chance on the pill?''

''No. There's no reason. I...''

Rafe swore and pushed himself to a sitting position. Then he ran his hand through his hair and looked at her. "If anything happens, I'll give you child support."

That was the last thing Shannon wanted to hear. She could believe Rafe hadn't come to the barn tonight with the intention of this happening. They had both gotten swept away. But she was romantic enough to believe that they'd been swept away because they cared deeply about each other. She didn't want child support. She wanted Rafe's love.

How could she have been so foolish to believe he might come to love her?

Quickly she fished her bra out from under her, slipped it on and fastened it, then grabbed her blouse and buttoned it. "If anything happens, I'll take responsibility for my child on my own. You don't have to worry, Rafe. I won't make any claims on you."

In record speed she slipped into her panties and then her jeans.

"I take my responsibilities seriously, Shannon."

"I never want to be anybody's responsibility." Sliding into her boots, she knew her pride would protect her, as it always had. "This was a mistake we can't undo. But we don't have to dwell on it, either. Just forget about what happened, Rafe, because I will."

Then she left the stall and the barn, hurrying to the house, to the safety of the life she'd built for herself.

Cars steadily flowed into the Rocky R on the third Sunday afternoon in July. Adjusting the brim of the black Stetson he'd bought in town last week, Rafe realized he was already comfortable with it. He watched Shannon mingle, talking to parents and kids, avoiding him whenever she could, just as she had for

the past two weeks. Nothing had changed in her demeanor and her caring for his daughter. In fact, she
had consulted with him twice about what had come
up in Janine's play therapy sessions. His daughter
wouldn't pick up or play with the mother doll, and
Shannon believed she was still blocking out her
mother's death. Still, other then Janine's welfare and
mundane conversation, he and Shannon had hardly
spoken.

And dammit, he missed her.

He'd never in his life lost control as he had that
night in the barn. He'd never before put pleasure in
front of good sense and a damn-the-consequences attitude that had gotten men into trouble from the beginning of time. What *would* he do if Shannon was
pregnant? He didn't want marriage, and she didn't
want a man taking care of his child out of duty. A
stalemate.

He'd cross that particular bridge when he came to
it.

Shannon had called a friend to help her with the
kids today while she spoke with their parents. She'd
shared an office with Marianne Whittaker in Sacramento before moving to the Rocky R. While Janine
happily took part, Marianne supervised relay games in
the yard in back of the house with the eight or so
children who had gathered there. Clancy moved about
the corral and pasture, giving smaller children rides on
Marigold. Shannon had enlisted him to manage the
horses while parents examined the mounts their children would be riding. He seemed to have a sense of
pride that Shannon had asked him to do something so
important. One afternoon when Clancy's foster father
had arrived early to pick him up, Rafe had talked to

Jim for a while and learned that Clancy had been in and out of five foster homes. He'd never known his father, and his mother had died of a drug overdose. But he seemed to be headed in the right direction now. Rafe hadn't caught him smoking again. Maybe his warning had done some good.

Over the past two weeks Rafe had built picnic tables and benches to use in the pavilion. He'd put a coat of paint on Marigold's shed and made repairs in and around the barn. Shannon had given up trying to dissuade him from helping with the chores, because she knew he needed to keep busy.

The sound of a truck coming down the lane made Rafe glance at it. When he did, he thought he recognized it. Jordy Donneker. What was *he* doing here? More trouble?

He headed toward the barn where Shannon stood with a few parents. After telling them to go ahead and have a look around, she excused herself from the group and headed toward the spot where Jordy had parked.

Rafe strode up beside her. "You don't have to talk to him. And if he makes trouble—"

"I invited him to bring Krissie here today."

"You what?"

"It'll be okay, Rafe. I have to get this settled." The sunshine glimmered on blond strands in Shannon's curls. Her ponytail bobbed as she walked, and he longed to tug on it like a school kid and then pull her into his arms. But they'd crossed the line when they'd had sex and that had changed everything between them.

"How are you going to settle anything with a man

who won't listen to reason?'' His voice was sharper than he intended.

''I'm hoping I can help him see reason today. It's a gamble, but I'm hoping it'll work.''

Jordy sauntered over to them, his daughter, a nine-year-old with straight brown hair and glasses, a few steps behind.

''I'm glad you could come today,'' Shannon said amiably, and then gave her attention to Krissie. ''The kids are playing games up behind the house. Do you think you'd like to join them?''

The child looked up at her father.

''I didn't come here for her to play games,'' Jordy said. ''You sounded like you wanted to settle things.''

''I do. But I want to make you a deal.''

Rafe spotted Cora coming toward them and wondered if she thought Shannon needed help, too.

Shannon just smiled at her aunt. ''Aunt Cora, would you take Krissie over to Marianne so she can join in the fun?''

''Sure thing.'' She motioned to the little girl. ''Come on. I think they're having a three-legged race.''

Again, Krissie looked up at her dad. He frowned, but nodded for her to go ahead, and the little girl happily took off beside Cora.

''What's the deal?'' Jordy asked.

''Before you brought Krissie to me, her grades were down. According to her teacher that wasn't her only problem. She wasn't playing with the other children, she didn't answer in class and she seemed to be afraid to try anything new.''

''She's always been quiet,'' Jordy snapped.

''She was more than quiet, Mr. Donneker. She was

afraid of her own shadow. What I started to do was give her confidence in herself. I think that was beginning to make a difference. Have you spent much time with her since she stopped therapy?''

He shrugged. ''Not much. She's with a sitter when I go to work. Sometimes she's in bed when I get home. Don't go sayin' I gotta spend more time with her. I can't. When I can work, I've gotta' work.''

''It's what you do and what you say when you're with her that counts,'' Shannon said nonaccusingly.

''I didn't come here for no advice.''

Rafe didn't know where Shannon got her patience. This man had to be pushing her to the limits of it.

''Since you haven't spent much time with her lately, all I ask is that you watch her this afternoon while you're here,'' Shannon offered. ''Watch her play with the other kids. Watch how she reacts to the horses and the kittens and Buster. Then you tell me if you don't see a difference in your daughter. If you honestly don't, just say so, and I'll give you back your money.''

Jordy stared at Shannon as if trying to figure out what game she was playing, but he must have seen that she was sincere. ''All right,'' he agreed. ''She's never played with other kids too well. She always sits off by herself and watches. Just the same, I don't see what that has to do with her gettin' higher grades.''

''If she's more confident in her ability to learn, if she's not afraid to make mistakes and get involved and give answers, I think her grades will go up. It won't happen overnight, and she might need you to show some interest in her schoolwork and in her.''

''You givin' me advice again?''

''I'm telling you what you have to do to help your daughter.''

He was silent for a few moments, then pulled his hat farther down on his head. "I'll go have a look and see what she's doin'."

As Jordy Donneker stalked off, Rafe turned to Shannon. "Even if he does see changes, he still might ask for his money back. What if your other clients think they can do the same thing?"

"I don't know. I do know I had to settle this in a way that was good for my reputation *and* that saved his pride."

Their gazes locked. "A man's pride is everything," Rafe agreed.

"A woman's is, too," she murmured, looking up at him as if she didn't want this wall between them any more than he did.

Another car came rolling down the lane. This wasn't the time or place to talk about what had happened in the barn. He'd decided it was best to get through the next three weeks and then go back to his life in Salinas. But seeing the emotion in Shannon's eyes now, feeling the visceral tug toward her, he wondered if he'd been wrong.

A group of parents came out of the barn and walked toward them. No point in starting something now they couldn't finish. "I'm going to light the charcoal and get the burgers and hot dogs ready."

"You've already done enough. The picnic tables are great. Cora and I can watch the burgers."

Her denial that she needed him, in any way, was almost as bad as Nancy needing him too much. "Someday, Shannon, you're going to have to accept the fact that you need help once in a while. I'll handle the barbecuing. You handle the parents and kids."

With startling clarity he suddenly realized that

Shannon needing him would be very different from Nancy needing him. He wouldn't mind charging in like a white knight now and then for Shannon. He wouldn't mind it at all.

A few hours later Rafe was surprised at the number of people who had come and gone during the course of the day. Some were Shannon's clients or former clients, others were curious about the type of therapy she did. Some stayed for the barbecue, others didn't. But most seemed impressed with the Rocky R. The biggest surprise of all was that Jordy Donneker and Krissie were still lingering as Rafe repositioned the smoldering coals in the grill. With the dusk, toasting marshmallows and singing songs seemed a good way to end the day. He'd found a peace on the Rocky R he'd never felt anywhere else. Maybe Donneker had felt it, too.

Rafe took a seat on the ground beside Shannon. Janine was hopping up and down with the other kids as they toasted marshmallows and waited for them to cool, then popped them into their mouths. He noticed that Donneker started out toasting Krissie's marshmallows for her, but after a while he let her do it herself.

The woman beside Shannon rose to her feet and went to one of the picnic tables in the pavilion to pour herself more soda. Then she sat there to chat with another parent.

Rafe leaned close to Shannon until their shoulders were brushing. "You've accomplished what you set out to do today."

She glanced up at him. "I hope so. I'm glad I sent a notice to the Sacramento paper. I had several parents from there."

Janine came over to them then and held out her long fork, offering them each a marshmallow.

"Have you had enough?" Shannon asked with a smile.

Janine nodded.

Shannon took the golden-toasted marshmallow from the fork and popped it into her mouth. Rafe did the same thing. Their gazes collided as they ate the sweet treats, and it seemed there were so many unsaid words between them. They'd made surface conversation today, as they had for the past two weeks. But there was so much emotion roiling beneath the surface. Shannon licked the sweet gooey candy from her finger, and Rafe remembered her lips on his body, her tongue on his skin.

Janine took her fork over to a picnic table and positioned it across the corner. Then she came back to Shannon and sat beside her, leaning into her. As the night shadows fell over the gathering, Rafe saw Shannon put her arm around his daughter's shoulders, bringing her close. If she ever *did* have a child, she would be a wonderful mother.

The kind of mother you'd like for Janine?

That thought slugged him in the gut.

A mother for Janine meant a wife for him. Somehow he would make it up to his daughter for not having a mother. Somehow they would manage. Since he'd been at the Rocky R, he'd realized how unfulfilling his marriage had been for him, even though he'd loved Nancy deeply. He'd always taken responsibility seriously. Coupled with the commitment to love for a lifetime, it became a great burden that colored everything a man did. He didn't want that burden ever again.

Shannon and Marianne began a round of "Row, Row, Row Your Boat." One song led into the next until it was almost nine-thirty when the group broke apart. Shannon had set up Tiki torches around the pavilion area. As Rafe dumped and doused the coals, the guests used flashlights she'd provided to find their way into the backyard, where light from the house illuminated their way. Janine had gone up with Cora and Marianne already.

Jordy Donneker approached Shannon, looking uncomfortable as he shifted from one foot to the other.

To give them some privacy, Rafe busied himself, taking the torches out of the ground. Still, he overheard Donneker finally say, "Krissie played with the other kids today."

"Yes, she did. She even seemed to be having a good time."

"I still don't see what that has to do with learnin'. But I guess if you and her teacher says it does, maybe I should give you another chance."

After a pause Shannon advised him, "Give it some thought. If you want to meet with me and Krissie's teacher to figure out what's best for her, we can do that, too."

After Jordy started off with Krissie toward the house, Rafe blew out the last candle and pulled it out of the ground. Then he gathered them up and picked up a flashlight. "You've made a convert."

"Maybe. If I can get him involved with Krissie and teach him how to be less critical, they'll both be a lot happier."

Suddenly alone with Shannon, the stars twinkling above and the scent of pine all around them, Rafe couldn't help asking, "And what will make *you* happy?"

She was silent for a few moments but then answered, "Having a husband someday to share all this with me. Having children that reflect all the good things we see in each other."

It wasn't what he'd expected. But now knowing Shannon's background, he realized how that might be her dream.

"Marriage isn't like that," he said matter-of-factly. "It's about two people seeing each other as they really are and somehow going on, anyway."

"I don't understand why it can't be both," she said softly.

His response was automatic. "That's because you've never been married."

"No, I never have."

An owl hooted in the night. The sound of car doors closing sliced through the hush. He was sorry he'd brought this up. He was sorry he was feeling more than desire for Shannon Collins.

In three weeks he'd be back in Salinas where he belonged.

Although Shannon was concentrating on Janine riding Marigold around the corral at a trot, she was very aware that Rafe had come to watch them. Last night she'd taken a monumental risk. Removing herself from him the past two weeks had been more difficult than anything she'd ever had to do. Last evening, when he'd asked what would make her happy, she'd known instantly she wanted to love him and she wanted him to love her. But she couldn't just blurt that out, so she'd gone about it in a roundabout way.

He'd backed off. He'd closed down the subject as if it was too hot to handle. She supposed it was if he was still grieving for Nancy. On the other hand, he'd made it sound as if his marriage had been less than he'd expected, that his commitment to his wife had seemed like a trap.

Shannon truly believed that when two people were meant to be together, they'd be whole in a way they couldn't be alone. That was the way she'd felt after she'd made love with Rafe.

He'd obviously not felt the same way.

After a week of riding Marigold with a saddle, Janine looked like a little pro. She was altogether comfortable with Marigold now, anywhere around her, sitting on top of her, leading her, grooming her. A little too comfortable. By the end of the week, Shannon would introduce Janine to a larger pony. A change. A world viewed from higher up. Change could bring out emotions in Janine that they needed to explore.

After Janine dismounted and helped Shannon unsaddle the pony, Rafe came into the corral. "Who would you like me to exercise this afternoon?"

Most afternoons while she saw Janine in the office, Rafe took out one of the horses.

"Rock-A-Bye could use a workout."

"Rock-A-Bye it is." They stood there for a few moments, as if they wanted to say more to each other but couldn't find the words. Rafe offered, "I'll help Janine groom Marigold if you want to go back to your office before your next client arrives."

"Thanks. I need to make some notes on the morning sessions."

As Rafe led Marigold over to her own corral, Shannon went to her office, her throat tightening, tears much too near the surface. She was letting her feelings for Rafe get to her. For the past week tears had come too easily. She'd been unusually tired, too. But that was because she wasn't sleeping well. She was dreaming of him.

As soon as Shannon stepped into her outer office, she saw Cora on the phone, looking very upset. Her aunt said into the receiver, ''I'll try to be there this afternoon.''

When she finished the conversation and hung up, Shannon asked, ''What's wrong?''

''It's Polly Ludwig. You know, my friend in Sacramento.'' Polly had worked with her aunt for ten years, and they were close friends.

''What's wrong?''

''She was hanging draperies last night when the step stool tipped over and she fell. She broke her arm and bumped her head, too, and the doctor won't let her go home without someone to be there to watch her. She just needs me to help her out for the next couple of days. Can you spare me?''

''Of course I can. Does she want you to pick her up at the hospital?''

''As soon as I can get there.'' Cora pushed away from the desk and stood. ''Are you sure you'll be okay here?''

''I'll be fine. What do you need to do before you leave?''

''Just pack, I guess.''

''Do you need help?''

''Sure. You can toss all my cosmetics into my travel bag while I get my clothes.''

Less than a half hour later Cora was almost ready. She was gathering together a crewelwork picture she was in the midst of sewing, along with her yarns and needles.

Shannon picked up her aunt's suitcase and travel bag. "I'll take these out to the truck for you."

"Are you sure you won't need it the next few days?"

"No. I can use your car. If it won't start, maybe Rafe will lend me his. The truck's more reliable, and I'll feel better knowing you have it."

Cora hadn't packed a lot, so her travel bag and suitcase weren't very heavy. The office screen door slammed shut behind Shannon as she went down the steps and crossed to the area near the house where her truck was parked. She set the travel bag and suitcase down by the passenger door for a moment, opened the door and put the suitcase inside on the floor. When she heard a sound, she turned.

Janine was flying toward her, running as fast as her little legs would carry her. She looked terribly upset. Rafe was close behind her, calling, "Janine," while Buster ran at his heels.

Shannon quickly put the travel bag inside on the seat and slammed the door. But when she did, she heard Janine yell, "No!"

Shannon went perfectly still at that one-syllable word, and she realized Janine had spoken aloud for everyone to hear.

Chapter Twelve

A moment later Shannon dropped to her knees and enveloped the little girl in her arms. "What's wrong, honey?"

From the tears coursing down Janine's face, it was obvious that that one word had been wrung from her. She wasn't saying anything else. Shannon thought about what had happened and then took a guess. "Did you think I was leaving?"

Janine looked from her father to Shannon and then solemnly nodded.

Rafe had hunkered down beside his daughter, too. "She saw you up here and just took off. I didn't know what was wrong."

Shannon squeezed Janine's shoulders. "I'm not going anywhere. Cora's leaving for a few days, that's all. Then she'll be back."

Apparently Shannon's words weren't reassuring to

Janine. She turned away from the two adults and dropped her head, sobs wracking her small body. Shannon knew there was more going on than Janine glimpsing a couple of suitcases. She put her arms around the seven-year-old again and held her tight. Janine's tears flowed faster than any river, her little body shook, and Shannon could feel the deep grief that had been buried far down deep inside, rising to the surface.

Rafe looked on with a frustrated expression, and Shannon knew he was feeling everything his daughter was…and probably more.

Time passed inconsequentially as Shannon knelt on the ground, hugging Janine, murmuring that it was all right, trying to let her embrace convey her love and her sympathy.

Eventually Janine's sobs turned into small hiccups, and the flow of her tears ebbed.

When Shannon leaned away, she gave her some room. "Can you tell me why you're so upset?" she asked, requesting the little girl to talk for the first time since she set foot on the ranch.

But Janine stayed silent.

"I think you're upset because you thought I was leaving. I also think you're upset because your mommy left you, and you didn't even have a chance to say goodbye."

Janine's tears began flowing again, and she came to Shannon, burying her head in her shoulder. Her little nod and her tight arms around Shannon's neck proved she'd hit the nail on the head.

Rafe's voice was gruff when he spoke. "She hasn't cried since Nancy died."

Over and over again Shannon stroked Janine's hair. "Your mommy knows you miss her."

At that, Janine pushed away from Shannon again and looked deep into her eyes, as if searching for the truth. Shannon tapped Janine's small chest. "Your mommy is never going to really leave you, if you have her in your heart. And I believe that wherever heaven is, she's looking down on you and watching over you."

Janine's eyes were filled with questions.

"We can talk about this anytime you want," Shannon encouraged her. "You can talk to your dad about it, too. He misses your mommy as much as you do."

Janine looked over at Rafe then, and he held out his arms to his daughter. "Come here. Give me a hug."

She went to him willingly, and Shannon breathed a sigh of relief. Janine wasn't shutting either of them out. Maybe now she could actually let both of them in.

"I miss your mommy very much," he said hoarsely. "Maybe you and I can help each other remember her."

When Janine pushed away from Rafe, she swiped her palms over her cheeks. Then she pointed to the swing in the backyard.

"Go ahead," Rafe said. "I want to talk to Shannon, then I'll come push you."

When Janine ran toward the swing, he shook his head. "She just switched everything off again. Should I pursue it?"

"We'll have to let *her* lead the way, but I think she's had enough for now."

"She spoke," he said, his voice deep and gravelly.

"Yes, she did. It's a good sign."

"Why won't she talk to me?" His voice was anguished.

"Because she can't tell you what she's feeling. She can't tell you the horror of what she saw. She can't deal with having to put any of it into words. That doesn't mean she won't."

He raked his hand through his hair. "Where's Cora going?"

"She's going to help a friend for a few days who had an accident."

More than anything Shannon wanted to ask Rafe if he was all right. She wanted to take away the pain in his eyes and somehow assure him that Janine would be whole again. But she couldn't do that now, with her feelings for him so very close to the surface. It would be too easy to tell him she loved him...too difficult to see the look in his eyes that said he didn't love her.

Cora came out of the office then, a tapestry bag in her hand, crossed the lane and the grass, approaching the truck.

Shannon was grateful for the interruption and checked her watch. "I don't have any more clients, and I'll have supper together in about an hour. Is that all right?"

Rafe's gaze went to his daughter, and he said absently, "That's fine." Then he strode off toward Janine, and Shannon knew nothing else was on his mind.

Only his daughter.

After supper Shannon went on a trail ride with Rafe and Janine. She wanted to keep an eye on the little girl. Rafe's daughter was more sober than she'd been the past few weeks, and Shannon wished she could read her mind. Was she processing? Was she accepting what Shannon had told her? In therapy tomorrow they would work on all of it. Shannon just wanted Janine to know she was here for her tonight if she needed her.

It was almost dark when they came back from their ride, and by the time they'd unsaddled the horses and groomed them, it was Janine's bedtime. When Shannon offered her a snack of milk and cookies, she refused it. But then she took Shannon's hand and tugged her toward the stairs.

Rafe looked directly at his daughter and pushed a little. "Do you want Shannon to help put you to bed tonight?"

Shannon knew he was hoping for a word. A simple "yes." Anything. Janine simply nodded.

After he let out a patient sigh, he glanced at Shannon. "Okay. I guess it's time for bed, then."

As Buster jumped up onto the bed and lay at its foot, Shannon read Janine a story. But then Janine wanted her dad to read one, too. Shannon had been sitting at Janine's left side on the bed, and now Rafe sat on the right. As he read one of her Dr. Seuss favorites, Shannon hurt deep inside as she listened to him change his voice with each character, trying to make his daughter smile. He did, once, and she saw the look on his face that told her Janine's smile was his favorite gift in all the world.

It felt so much as if they were a family, sitting here like this. But they weren't.

After they tucked Janine in, then kissed her goodnight, Rafe descended the steps with Shannon.

In the living room she asked, "How about a glass of iced tea?"

He shook his head. "Could that one word today have been a shot in the dark? *Will* she be talking again soon?"

Shannon knew what he wanted her to say. But she couldn't. "I don't know that any more than you do."

"You're the therapist!" His impatience and frustration were palpable.

"Yes, I am. But I'm not a mind reader."

"In three weeks I'll be leaving to go back to Salinas and put our lives back together, one way or the other. If I'm not here, will she pull away from me even more?"

Reflexively Shannon took a few steps closer to him. "Not if you keep in touch. Not if you call her every night and come up on weekends." Reaching out, she touched his arm. "Janine needs you, Rafe, as much as she needs me."

Her hand on his arm, her skin against his, was the connection she'd been avoiding and he'd been avoiding since they'd made love. When she realized how ever present and alive the scorching desire between them still was, she pulled her hand back. She would have moved away, too, but suddenly his hands were on her shoulders, and the intense green fire in his eyes kept her pinned to the spot.

"Shannon," he murmured.

She could see that he needed her as much as she needed him. She couldn't deny either of them.

His arms circled her, bringing her tight against him. She could feel the essential want, the deep hunger that had burned between them since her eyes had first met his. She gave herself up to the taut heat of his lips, and when his mouth opened over hers, she let him sweep her away to that place where she was beautiful and desired and totally in love.

Abruptly his tongue withdrew, and he broke the kiss. "Do you understand what I want from you?" he rasped.

She did. All too well. He wanted the night and pleasure with no commitments or strings and no recriminations in the morning. She could give that to him as long as he was here. She could give him her love. Maybe it would make a difference. "Yes," she murmured, knowing full well what she was doing.

When he kissed her again, there was a difference about this one. It was possessively slow, deliberately seductive and altogether consuming. When he pulled away and trailed kisses across her cheek to her ear, he said, "I'm prepared tonight. I have my wallet in my jeans."

Even in her passion-drugged haze, she knew he was talking about condoms. Their wild lovemaking the first time had led to unprotected sex. That was unusual for Rafe, she suspected. He used reasoning and logic and control the same way she used intuition. He didn't like to be caught unprepared. Tonight he wasn't.

Startling her, he scooped her up into his arms. "Let's go to your room."

In her bedroom a few moments later he set her down by the bed and switched on her table lamp. "I want to see you."

Just his words made her tremble.

When Rafe tugged her T-shirt from her jeans, she lifted her arms, and he pulled it over her head. Then he slowly traced the fabric of her bra above her breasts. "This happened too fast the last time. It's not going to happen that way tonight."

Although their first time together had caused separation between them until now, she had to tell him how special it had been. "It might have been fast. But...it was the first time I ever climaxed."

He didn't speak, just stroked the skin above her breasts with a reverence that almost brought tears to her eyes. "We'll see how much better we can make this one," he finally said, as he reached around her and unhooked her bra.

When his gaze lingered on her freed breasts, she felt as if he were actually touching her. Then he was, and it was so much better than having him simply look at her. The pads of his thumbs were slightly rough, and they rimmed her nipple, driving her crazy.

She felt her knees going weak. "Rafe..."

"Let's get the rest of your clothes off," he growled. "Then I can touch you the way I've wanted to touch you from the first moment I saw you in the barn."

"I want to touch you, too," she said.

"Being that damn honest isn't always a virtue," he warned her with a crooked grin.

"Why not?"

"Because I'm so hard I feel like I'm going to explode."

"I want to touch you there, too."

This time he groaned and unsnapped her jeans. A few minutes later they were lying naked on her bed, facing each other. Rafe slid his hand under her hair and nudged her to him. Then he took her lower lip between his teeth and laved it slowly.

She began trembling again, and he noticed. "You're the most sensual woman I've ever met."

Questions about his marriage flooded through her...about his sex life with his wife.

Perceptively he said, "I was faithful in my marriage, Shannon. But Nancy... My hunger scared her, so I kept it in check."

Shannon had wanted to touch Rafe for so long she couldn't imagine not wanting to do it. His hunger and intensity were facets of him that she loved. She drew her hand down his chest, hesitated in the soft hair above his navel only a moment, and then she cupped him. "I want your hunger, Rafe. I need it."

"And I need yours." He slid his hand between her legs then, and kissed her with fire and need and all of his hunger, not holding back at all.

His kiss and desire created a burst of sensation inside of her that left her quivering and ready for him.

Shannon felt open to Rafe in a way she'd never felt open to another human being. As he caressed and stroked her, she kissed him back, moaned her pleasure and tried to give him as much pleasure as he was giving her. Their bodies became slick with their desire. Their breathing became ragged. Their hearts beat as one.

When Rafe reached to his jeans on the floor, he pulled out his wallet and a foil packet inside. She watched as he tore it open, but then she took it from his hands, rolled it onto him and heard his breath catch.

Then he rose above her. That's when she opened her heart completely to him. That's when he slid into her with a provocative sensuality that stole all the breath from her lungs. She clung to his broad shoulders and took him deeper inside of her.

He entered and withdrew, entered and withdrew, until she was begging him to stay, not only inside of her, but in her life. The plea was silent, but she hoped he could feel it…hoped he knew how deeply she loved him.

With each of Rafe's driving thrusts, she began a slow, steep climb to the summit of a mountain. Each stroke took him deeper. Each stroke took her higher…until she could almost see forever. When she reached the crest of the summit, she teetered there for a few mind-shattering seconds, until his final thrust propelled her into the clouds—into a universe of sparkling colors, brilliant feelings, liquid sensations. She clung to him until a few seconds later, when his guttural groan and the spasms shuddering through his body told her he'd soared off the mountain with her. They hung suspended, as glorious waves of incandescent pleasure bathed them time and time again.

After a slow, lazy descent from the sublime, Rafe rolled to his side, opened his eyes and gazed at her. He brushed her hair from her cheek, and she was sure she saw deep caring in his eyes. "Can you stay?" she asked.

He hugged her to him. "For a little while. I wouldn't want Janine to wake up, need me and find me gone."

Shannon nestled farther into his shoulder, loving the scent of him, the strength of him. She fell asleep in his arms, never having felt more protected…more safe…or more loved.

When Shannon awakened, Rafe was gone. She'd fallen asleep in his arms so easily, as if she belonged there. Now as the new day dawned, she thought about last night all over again. She smiled…until she thought about him leaving.

She wouldn't think about that.

After taking a shower, she dressed, and as she came out of her bedroom she smelled coffee brewing.

When she entered the kitchen, Rafe was standing by the coffeepot, a mug in his hand. In a black T-shirt and jeans, he was more rugged and handsome than any man she'd ever known. But then, she was so in love with him her toes almost curled just thinking about it.

"Hi," he said with a smile that told her he remembered everything about last night as well as she did.

"Hi," she returned somewhat uncertainly, not knowing what to expect this morning.

Setting down his coffee mug, he crossed to her. "Any regrets?"

She shook her head.

"Good." Then he took her in his arms and gave her a kiss she could savor for weeks.

Finally he broke the kiss and leaned away. "Do you have a full schedule today?"

"Yes. And I want to spend some extra time with Janine. Yesterday was a breakthrough, and I want to take advantage of it."

"While you're busy with your other clients, I'll take her into town and we'll get supplies for ice cream again."

"That sounds good."

He dragged his thumb down her cheek. "I'm not a game player, Shannon, so I'm just going to ask you this outright. After Janine goes to bed, I'd like to spend some time with you again."

"In bed?"

He gave her a slow smile. "We could start out necking on the couch while we watch TV."

"Or we could start out necking on the porch

swing," she suggested amiably, aware of the trail of heat on her cheek.

"The porch swing, the sofa, the floor. I don't care. As long as the end result's the same. I want you, Shannon."

She was feeling all quivery inside again and knew there was something she could do to make their time together even more pleasurable. She had a block of time free tomorrow. Maybe her doctor could see her and measure her for a diaphragm.

Before she could even suggest it to Rafe, he was kissing her again, and she was forgetting about everything but being held in his arms.

When Shannon returned from her doctor's appointment Wednesday afternoon, she saw her truck parked on the gravel and knew Cora was back. Rafe had insisted she take his car to drive into Fawn Grove, and she had. It drove like a dream. When she'd told him why she was going into town, he'd said, "You don't have to do that."

"But," she'd explained, "I want to." He'd kissed her then, with all of the explosive passion they experienced every time they came together.

For the past two days her work with Janine had been concentrated on getting her emotions out. The seven-year-old had finally drawn the scene in the restaurant. She'd cried again, but she still hadn't spoken. Shannon knew it would take patience and plenty of time, but they'd get there. She was sure of it.

Shannon couldn't help humming her favorite song as she climbed the porch steps, swinging her pharmacy bag. Rafe was in the kitchen, pouring himself a glass of iced tea. When he spotted her, he didn't smile.

"I see Cora's back," she said conversationally.

"About fifteen minutes ago. Janine went over with her to help her unpack her suitcases. She said she had something for her."

Lifting her bag, Shannon said, "And I have something for us."

Still, Rafe didn't smile. "Constantine called."

"What did he want?"

"Something about a benefit dinner on Sunday. He seems to think you're going with him. He said you should call him so you can finalize your plans."

Now she could easily see Rafe was jealous. She would be, too, if he went to dinner with another woman. "I never said I'd go with Nolan. We both have tickets, and I told him I'd probably see him there. That's all. It's not a date."

Rafe took a few swallows of iced tea, eyed her over the glass, then set it on the counter. "What kind of benefit is it?"

"There's a women's shelter in Fawn Grove. This is one of the ways they make money every year."

He thought about that for a few seconds. "Can I still get a ticket?"

"I imagine so. Are you sure you want to go?"

"Would you like an escort?"

She said what was in her heart. "If that escort is you."

His jaw didn't seem quite so set when he came over to her. "I would guess this charity is important to you."

"It is."

"Does Constantine know why?"

She shook her head. "I've only ever told Marianne

and Cora and my mentor in college about my background.''

''The people you're closest to.''

''Yes.''

''You don't consider yourself close to Constantine?''

''Not in the same way I'm close to you.''

After studying her for a moment, Rafe wrapped his arms around her and brought her into his chest. It always felt so good to be held in his embrace.

''I've been thinking,'' he murmured into her hair.

''What about?'' Her hopes rose. Maybe he was going to stay longer. Maybe he was coming to care for her more deeply....

''I think you should give back Constantine's money.'' His words penetrated the warmth of his embrace, and she pushed away.

''What?''

''Get clear of Constantine. Let me fund the indoor ring.''

''I can't let you do that.''

''Why?''

''Because I already told Nolan I'd accept his contribution.''

''So, tell him differently.''

''No! There are no strings with Nolan. With you, I...'' She didn't know quite how to say it. She was in love with Rafe. Yet he wasn't in love with her. She couldn't accept his money. It would seem like a payment of some sort.

''Do you think I'd want control over what you'd do with the money?''

''I don't know. I just know I don't want to take money from you.''

"I'm paying you for Janine's therapy."

"That's different. We made those arrangements before—"

"Before we went to bed together?"

She wouldn't put it that way. But it was essentially true. "Yes."

"So if we hadn't slept together, you'd accept the money?"

"I don't know. I just know that being involved with you and accepting money from you don't go together."

Knowing Shannon's background, Rafe could understand that she didn't want any man to have control of her life. Was she letting Constantine give the donation because she felt he was safe?

Rafe knew whenever he saw Shannon with Constantine, or thought about Shannon with Constantine, he was jealous. And he had no right to be. He had no right to want any say in her life, because he wouldn't be sticking around. Investing himself in a committed relationship again would be just too difficult. Too complicated. Too risky.

"If you change your mind, or if Constantine decides there are unseen strings attached to his money, my offer will hold." He didn't have to be involved with Shannon to support her work. After he left, she would spend her life helping children. He knew that.

"I don't need your money, Rafe." She gazed into his eyes as if she was looking for something. "But I'd love to have you with me on Sunday."

"If Cora can sit with Janine, you've got it."

"I'll check with her and then call Nolan back."

"And tell him..."

"That you asked me to go with you and I said yes

because we want to spend time together before you leave.''

She made it sound so rational. And it was. But deep inside he didn't like the idea of leaving—any more than he liked her calling back Nolan Constantine.

Chapter Thirteen

On Saturday afternoon after Shannon had seen her last client, she changed into her bathing suit in her bedroom, feeling unreasonably happy. Last night she and Rafe had made love until well after one, then napped a little before he'd gone up to his bedroom. She wished she could spend all night in his arms, but she understood his need to be upstairs for his daughter. Today she'd promised Janine she would go swimming with her and her dad at the neighbor's pond. She loved spending time with both of them. This new closeness she felt with Rafe gave her hope that he was feeling it, too.

Picking up her tropical-design kimono that coordinated with her black-and-flowered one-piece bathing suit, she slipped on a pair of sandals and went down the hall. When she'd almost reached the living room, she could hear Rafe's voice, and realized he was speaking into his cell phone.

"Cover the same services you performed last month," Rafe directed, "dusting and vacuuming, washing the floors and counters in the kitchen and bathroom. I'll be home August fifth, so a few days before that will be fine. You might want to air out the house, too. It's been closed up for weeks." There was a pause, and then he responded, "Yes, it will be good to get home. Just leave your bill on the counter, Ruth, and I'll write you a check as soon as I get home."

Of course Shannon knew Rafe would be returning to Salinas and his house there. *Of course* she knew he'd be returning to his job—the one that offered an important promotion, a prestigious step up in his career. *Of course* she knew her time with him was limited and that all he expected from their nights in bed together was pleasure. No commitment. No strings. No future involvement.

In the core of her, where dreams were born and hope lived, she realized she'd been nurturing the possibility that Rafe did love her. Hearing him on the phone, and the relief in his voice when he said he was glad he'd be going home, hopes and dreams and possibilities withered into reality.

In the next two weeks she had to make herself accept the fact that Rafe Pierson would be leaving.

Taking a deep breath, she became determined to enjoy any time they had left and to make memories that would last a lifetime. Because she knew after loving Rafe, she'd never love another man again.

Fawn Grove's firehall included a community room where many social functions were held—senior center luncheons, holiday parties and charity events. Wedding receptions, too. Shannon steered away from that thought as Rafe opened the door to the community room on Sunday evening and let her precede him inside.

"You've been awfully quiet today," he commented as he positioned his hand on the small of her back, guiding her toward the other attendees.

She forced a smile. The truth was that ever since she'd overheard Rafe's phone call yesterday, an unyielding sadness had overtaken her. It was unlike her to dwell on things that she couldn't change. "I have a lot on my mind, I guess."

"This dinner. Choosing a builder for the ring. Finding another horse or two who'll be good with kids." Rafe's eyes probed hers, looking for anything else she wasn't telling him. But then he gave her a slow smile and brushed the back of his hand along her cheek. "Quite a serious list you have there."

"It'll all fall into place if I give it enough time." At least she was hoping that was true. After Rafe left and time passed, maybe she would feel less sad about losing her heart's desire.

He playfully touched the tip of her nose. "You have more freckles today than you did yesterday."

When she worked in the corral, she usually wore a hat in the sun. She had used sunscreen yesterday at the pond, but they'd had so much fun, splashing and dunking each other, that she'd gotten an extra dose of sun. "Before life on the Rocky R, I used to cover them with makeup."

"I like the natural look," he remarked as she and Rafe found two vacant seats at one of the long tables.

The woman to the right of Shannon smiled up at

her. "Hello. You're Shannon Collins, aren't you? I saw the article in the *Register* about the work you do with children and horses."

"That's me," Shannon responded. "And you're—"

The woman extended her hand to shake Shannon's. "I'm Helen McConnell. I own The New Woman, a boutique over on Pasedo and Fourth Street. I'm also on the board of directors for Safe Haven."

Shannon shook the woman's hand. "It's good to meet you."

Rafe had just pulled out Shannon's chair for her when Nolan came sauntering down the aisle. His usually bland expression was almost a scowl, and Shannon wasn't sure whether it was turned on her or Rafe. She'd phoned Nolan and told him that Rafe would be bringing her. He'd ended the conversation abruptly then and didn't look any too happy to see them together now.

Without preamble he said, "I was surprised you'd give your time to something like this, Pierson. After all, it's going to be another chicken dinner."

Rafe looked unperturbed. "I enjoy chicken—and Shannon's company even more. Besides, it's certainly a worthy cause I support."

"You don't even live in Fawn Grove."

"No. But that doesn't mean I can't support the charity."

"Won't you be returning to Salinas soon? So you can put all the bad guys in jail?"

Helen had been unabashedly following the conversation and now asked, "Are you a police officer?"

Shannon introduced Rafe to Helen and then added, "He's a D.A. in Salinas."

Helen gave him a sly smile. "A lawyer. How interesting. Are you here on vacation?"

"No," Rafe responded honestly. "Shannon is working with my daughter."

The smile slipped from Helen's lips as she obviously realized the seriousness of that. "I see. Well, if you have any free time while you're here, we could always use legal advice at the shelter."

"You don't have anyone on staff?"

"We can't afford that. But soon, I hope."

"I'd be glad to stop in this week."

Taking a card from her purse, Helen handed it to him. "Call me when you are free, and we'll set up a time."

Looking disgruntled at the direction of the conversation, Nolan asked Shannon, "Can I talk to you? In private?"

Shannon glanced at Rafe, but his expression didn't convey how he felt about it. She said to him, "I won't be long."

After a few additional words to Helen O'Connell, Rafe sat at the table and waited for Shannon to return. He told himself it really didn't matter what Constantine wanted with Shannon. But it *did* matter. As his gaze followed them to a quiet corner by a side entrance, he realized how difficult it would be to leave Janine with Shannon at the Rocky R. How difficult it would be not only to leave his daughter, but Shannon, too. He had no choice, really. He had to get his professional life back on track. Becoming D.A. was a serious proposition. Yet, where he once relished the idea, now he wasn't as enthusiastic about it. Had he lost his taste for the pursuit of justice? Or did he need a different avenue to pursue it? Or a different venue for practicing law?

The waitress brought Rafe his salad and set one at Shannon's place, too. A few minutes later Shannon made her way back to the table by herself. When she sat down beside Rafe, he asked, "What was that all about?"

Looking perturbed, she picked up her napkin. "Remember when you told me that Nolan's donation didn't come without strings?"

"Yes," Rafe drawled.

"Well, it might have come without strings. But he did it for a reason other than publicity for his stores...or even a tax write-off. He wanted to tell me there would be an announcement in tomorrow's paper. He'll be running for mayor of Fawn Grove in the fall."

"That surprises you?"

"I must seem naive," she said with a sigh.

"Not naive. You just want to see the good in everyone. That's okay."

When she turned and their eyes met, there was something in hers that caused his chest to tighten. He wasn't sure what it was. But he suddenly realized it would turn him inside out...if he'd let it. It would become that burden of responsibility mixed with heart-rending feeling. He couldn't let it.

During dinner he thought about returning to Salinas and everything he'd have to do when he got back. He went over what Sam had told him and considered how becoming D.A. would change his life. Most of all he distanced himself from the turmoil he felt whenever Shannon's gaze met his.

By the time the waitress served dessert, he'd decided that tonight he would turn in after Janine went to bed and leave Shannon alone. He'd prove to himself he didn't need Shannon Collins in his life. He'd prove to himself he didn't need any woman at all.

It was almost suppertime on Monday when Shannon left her office and headed for the corral. She was having trouble keeping her mind off what had happened last night...rather what *hadn't* happened last night. Rafe's attitude toward her had changed in the course of the evening at the firehall. After they'd returned home from dinner and put Janine to bed, he'd told Shannon, "Sam Patterson brought along a few cases he wants me to look over. I'll do that up in my room. See you at breakfast."

That's how their night had ended, and Shannon had wondered why Rafe was pulling away. Throughout a sleepless night she'd concluded he was severing the bonds between them because that would make it easier for him to leave. It was a very practical solution but one that hurt her deeply.

As Shannon approached the corral, she saw that Rafe and Janine were waiting for her. Since she'd spoken that one word last week, Janine had drawn pictures of her mommy for Shannon. In one of them Nancy had wings. Janine was slowly beginning to accept what had happened to her mother. In play therapy this morning she'd picked up the mother doll and put it in the house with the daddy and little girl. Her play was still silent, but Shannon knew they were making progress.

Hopefully this afternoon Cloppy could help Janine make even more progress.

Avoiding Rafe's gaze and her turmoil about him,

Shannon crouched down in front of Janine. "Instead of riding Marigold today, I'd like to give you a walk around the corral on Cloppy. What do you think?"

At first Janine looked startled they weren't following the regular routine. Then she looked frightened.

"The idea of riding Cloppy might seem a little scary, but you know how nice she is. She always nuzzles your neck after you feed her a carrot," Shannon reminded her.

Janine seemed to think about that.

Rafe spoke then. "I'll clean up Marigold's shed while you two are having your session." Giving Janine a reassuring smile, he ruffled her hair and then headed for the pony's corral. He was giving his daughter breathing space and Shannon room to work.

Concentrating on Janine, Shannon said conversationally, "I wish you could talk. Then you could tell me how you feel about riding Cloppy. It isn't always easy to guess what you're thinking."

When Janine didn't react, Shannon clasped the little girl's shoulder. "I know you're probably afraid because Cloppy is bigger than Marigold."

Janine nodded.

"But you also know how gentle she is. And I'll lift you so you can put your foot in the stirrup and slide your leg over. It won't be much different from riding Marigold, but you'll probably be able to see more. Come on. Let's go talk to Cloppy about it."

Inside the barn Janine petted the pony's nose. After a few minutes Shannon opened the stall door. "I'll saddle her up. You can help me. If you decide you don't want to ride her, we'll simply unsaddle her again."

When Janine didn't make any sign of protest, Shannon took hold of Cloppy's halter and led her out.

The seven-year-old brought Shannon a saddle blanket when she requested it, then watched soberly as Shannon cinched the girth of a light saddle. She wanted Janine to feel the horse under her.

Rafe's daughter walked with Shannon out to the corral, then looked up at the horse.

Standing in front of Cloppy, Shannon beckoned to Janine. "Come here and look into her eyes. See how kind she is. I think you know that already, but maybe she can convince you."

As Shannon requested, Janine stood before the horse, looking into her eyes. Then she tentatively brushed her finger over Cloppy's muzzle. The mare rubbed her nose over Janine's hand.

"Are we going to try it?" Shannon asked her little client.

When Janine nodded slowly, Shannon smiled and handed Janine her helmet. "Come on. Let me help you up."

After Janine adjusted the strap of the riding helmet, Shannon lifted her. She put her foot in the stirrup and took hold of Cloppy's mane, settling herself on top of the fourteen-hand horse.

"What do you think?" Shannon asked as she adjusted the break-away stirrups.

Janine's eyes were very wide and she still looked uneasy. But she gave a shrug, and Shannon took hold of Cloppy's lead to walk the pony around the corral.

About twenty minutes later, Rafe had finished with Marigold's shed and he came to stand at the corral, watching his daughter. Shannon felt his gaze also on her, and she wished she could say or do something to change everything between them. To open up Rafe to her love. But she couldn't. Only *he* could do that. Apparently he wasn't ready. She should have known that. She shouldn't have fallen in love with him. But this time she hadn't been able to prevent love from finding her and carrying her away.

After she led the pony close to Rafe, she scratched Cloppy between her ears. "I think that's enough for today. Cora will have supper ready soon."

"I don't want to go in yet."

Janine's simple declaration made Shannon's breath catch. The small voice was so unexpected, so sweetly childlike, so welcome to hear, that tears burned Shannon's eyes. Not wanting Janine to close up again, she knew she had to stay calm. She didn't dare glance at Rafe. Forcing a nonchalance she didn't feel, she responded, "We can probably ride another few minutes. Aunt Cora said she made dessert for tonight. What do you hope it is?"

Praying Janine would answer her, Shannon waited.

Janine looked over at her. "Brownies."

Shannon sensed rather than saw Rafe move then, until he was through the gate, standing beside Janine and Cloppy. He scooped his daughter into his arms and hugged her. "Peanut. I can't believe you're talking," he said, his voice thick with emotion.

Pushing away from his chest, Janine looked directly into his eyes. Then she smiled and touched his cheek. "Daddy."

Shannon saw Rafe's eyes glisten then, and hers were moist, too. This had to be an extraordinary moment for him as well as for Janine. She felt so much a part of it she wanted to wrap her arms around both of them. But she didn't know what Rafe wanted, and she wasn't sure what to do.

After he composed himself, Rafe gave his daughter another tight squeeze and set her back on top of the horse. During the next fifteen minutes or so, as Janine finished her ride, she didn't talk, and Shannon wondered if she was pulling back into her safe world again.

But after the three of them returned to the house, Janine went over to Cora. "Can I have a drink of water?"

Cora's startled expression soon became a wide smile.

Throughout the evening as they all sat on the porch and played crazy eights, Janine petted Buster and concentrated on the game. Once in a while she looked at her dad and smiled.

Shannon knew they still had work to do, but Rafe had gotten his daughter back.

This night when it was time for Janine to go to bed, she looked up into Shannon's face and asked, "Will you read me a story?"

Every time Janine spoke, Shannon was filled with such gratitude that she sent up a thank-you prayer.

After storytime, Buster jumped up onto the bed and Janine hugged Rafe. "Good night, Daddy." Then she hugged Shannon, too. "Good night, Shannon."

Shannon couldn't help placing a small, sweet kiss by Janine's temple. Her heart felt as if it were shaking and breaking and soaring all at the same time. Janine might not be leaving the Rocky R with her dad, but she would be leaving soon.

When Shannon went downstairs with Rafe, she

wasn't sure what to say. "You must be so relieved," she finally managed.

"Relieved? I'm not sure that's quite it. Grateful's more like it. I'm so very grateful to you, Shannon, for what you've done."

She didn't want his gratitude. She wanted something much more lasting. "It's my job."

He came within touching distance, then stopped and shook his head. "Janine isn't just a client to you. I can see that. Thank you for everything you've given her."

Tears welled up in Shannon's eyes. "She's given me a lot, too."

They stared at each other for long moments until Rafe gave a low oath and hauled her into his arms. "I can't be here and not want you. I thought if we didn't go to bed together again, that would make leaving easier. But I was wrong. I want you, Shannon. Every night we have until I leave."

Her heart was beating so fast she couldn't catch it. She hadn't thought she'd ever make love with Rafe again. Now she had the chance to love him once more.

She wanted to tell him how much she loved him, but she knew he couldn't accept that. So she murmured, "I want you, too."

Taking her face between his hands, he ran his thumbs up and down her cheeks. "I want to kiss you so badly I can't think straight. And if I kiss you, we'll be in your bed in two seconds flat. I want to get a shower first and make sure Janine's asleep."

She felt as if she could melt into his large, warm hands. She felt as if she could melt into him. But she could use a shower, too, and she had to put in her diaphragm.

"I'd suggest we shower together," he said with a grin, "but your shower's too small, and I'm afraid we'd make too much noise in the one upstairs." Then he sealed his lips to hers for a fast, quick kiss and released her.

It was difficult to find her voice, but she breathed, "I'll meet you in my bedroom."

Rafe gave her another quick, soul-stopping kiss, then went upstairs.

Feeling as if she were walking on a rainbow and might fall off at any time, Shannon went into her bathroom to ready herself for Rafe.

After she quickly showered, she had every intention of inserting the diaphragm before she dried her hair. The spermicidal jelly needed time to activate. It would, while she put lotion on her body, brushed her teeth and then let Rafe kiss her and touch her any place he pleased.

But suddenly she was standing at the sink with the pink case in her hand, overwhelmed by the desire *not* to use the diaphragm. She would love having Rafe's baby. What if she could get pregnant tonight? What if after Janine and Rafe were out of her life she'd still have a child to love?

The idea made Rafe's leaving seem bearable. The idea gave her hope and new purpose, and she realized just how much she wanted to be a mother.

She set the pink case on the corner of the sink, opened the medicine cabinet and took out her toothbrush and toothpaste, telling herself a child could make her feel as whole as loving Rafe.

Propped on his elbow an hour later, Rafe gazed down at Shannon, who was sleeping by his side. There was no way he could stay away from her until he left. No way at all.

Even now he didn't want to go back upstairs.

As he glanced into the hall, he realized the light there still shone. He would turn it off and then catch another hour of sleep with Shannon. He liked the feel of her in his arms, the soft, honeysuckle scent of her next to him.

Easing himself out of bed, he went to the door. He was about to switch off the light when he decided to get a drink in Shannon's bathroom. He went inside and turned on the light. He knew Shannon kept paper cups in the medicine cabinet.

When he opened the mirrored door, a tube of toothpaste tumbled out, landing on the pink plastic case on the sink, knocking it to the floor. The case popped open, and Rafe was stooping to retrieve it when he froze. It was Shannon's diaphragm case, and the diaphragm was still inside.

For a few moments he just stared at it, unable to believe his eyes. Why wasn't she using it? What was she trying to pull? Shannon wasn't dishonest. She was—

He didn't know *what* she was.

Angrily scooping up the case, leaving the toothpaste where it lay and the medicine cabinet door open, he strode down the hall and into the bedroom.

Shannon must have heard him coming because she opened her eyes and propped up on her elbows. "Rafe? Is everything all right?"

"Not a damn thing is all right. Why the hell aren't you using this?" He held out the case with the diaphragm in it.

Shannon paled.

Coming over to the side of the bed, he closed the case with a snap and threw it down on the nightstand. "What did you decide to do? Trap me?" His voice rose with fury.

"No!"

"I guess if you didn't decide to trap me, you decided to use me." He pointed to the nightstand with a wide wave of his arm. "Have you ever even used the damned thing? Have you?" His voice was loud, his question pointed. For a few seconds, he thought he saw fear in Shannon's eyes. Fear? Of him?

Swearing viciously, he took a step back. "I'm angry as hell, Shannon. But I would never, *ever* raise a hand to you. Don't you know that?"

"I didn't think you would. I..."

"I thought you were an honest woman, Shannon. I never thought you'd lie to me."

"I'm *not* lying. For an instant, just an instant..." Her voice broke. "I *know* you'd never hurt me, no matter how angry you are. Please believe me."

"Believe you? The same way I believed you when you said you were using your diaphragm? When we were in bed together, I thought you were protected."

"I was. I used it. It's just tonight—"

"I'm supposed to believe that? That tonight you decided, impulsively, not to use it? Why?"

His harsh question hung in the silence. Finally she answered him. "Because you're leaving. Because I had this insane wish that tonight I might get pregnant and I'd have—" She stopped abruptly. "It doesn't matter. I'm sorry, Rafe."

"Sorry because you got caught. Were you going to leave it in its case tomorrow night, too?"

"I hadn't thought that far ahead. You seemed to

pull away on Sunday, as if you wanted everything between us to end. And tonight when you said you wanted me again…'' She swept her hair away from her face. ''I…I just thought—''

''You used me, Shannon. You deceived me.''

He'd come down to Shannon's room tonight in his sleeping shorts. Now he grabbed them from the corner of the bed and put them on. ''I think Janine needs *me* around now as much as she needs you, or I'd go back to Salinas tomorrow. But I'm going to watch her progress carefully. By August fifth if not before, I think she'll be able to go home with me. You might want to start getting her ready for that.''

When he went to the door, he couldn't resist a parting shot. ''If you want to be inseminated by some man, try Nolan Constantine. You two use the same kind of tactics. Maybe you should consider being more than friends. Or was that a lie, too?''

Without giving her a chance to answer, he crossed the threshold and quickly strode down the hall. Shannon Collins might have helped his daughter, but she'd sent his already off-kilter world spinning. Tonight the spinning would stop.

By August fifth, he would have everything in his life in order again.

Chapter Fourteen

Thank goodness, the restroom at the Twin Pines family restaurant was empty when Shannon went inside, a pharmacy bag in her hand. For the past nine days she'd been heartsick about Rafe and couldn't begin to penetrate the wall he'd put up around himself. She'd made an impulsive, reckless decision that had destroyed any feelings he might have had for her. She didn't blame him for being angry and feeling betrayed, but she wished he'd given her a chance to explain that she'd wanted his child so desperately...because she couldn't have him.

But he wouldn't listen to her now. He wouldn't discuss anything personal, except Janine. Rafe might have shut her out, but ever since his daughter had begun talking again, Shannon had felt even closer to her. She'd managed to get Janine to talk to her about what had happened that day in the restaurant. As Janine had again sobbed in her arms, Shannon's heart had broken for her.

For the past few days she'd been preparing Janine to go back to her life in Salinas with her dad. Shannon would like to work with the seven-year-old a few weeks more, but she didn't have a few weeks. On Sunday Rafe and Janine would be gone.

Opening the white bag, Shannon took out the pregnancy test. She was more than a week late, and she was *never* late. She suspected if she was pregnant, it had happened the very first time she and Rafe had made love in the barn.

After she read the directions carefully, she followed them to the letter and then waited for the plus or minus sign to appear. What if she was pregnant? Should she tell Rafe? She wouldn't trap him or saddle him with a responsibility he didn't want. Yet, didn't he also have the right to know if he was going to be a father again?

When the plus sign appeared, it wasn't a shock to Shannon. The fatigue she'd been feeling, as well as her loss of appetite, should have alerted her sooner that her body was going through changes. But she'd been so caught up in everything that was happening. Loving Rafe. Helping Janine. Running the Rocky R.

She was going to have a baby. Rafe's child. What would be the best thing to do, for him and Janine and herself? Tears came to Shannon's eyes as she tried to sort through it and couldn't. Gathering up the pregnancy kit, she tossed all of it into the wastebasket under the counter. She only had a few days to decide whether she would raise this child alone without involving Rafe in any of it, or whether she would tell him she was having his baby.

Shannon forced herself to sit at a table at the Twin Pines to eat a sandwich and drink a glass of milk. In spite of everything, she had to do whatever was best for the baby. That meant eating right and taking care of herself, no matter how confused she was. She'd rearranged her appointments so she could have a couple of hours to herself this afternoon. Now she didn't know what to do with them, any more than she knew what to do about Rafe.

When she finished at the restaurant, she walked to a store that sold baby clothes, toys and almost anything a child would need. She wandered about, absently touching an infant seat, picking up a teddy bear, passing by five styles of strollers. She left the shop without making a purchase, thinking about what it would mean to be a single parent, knowing she couldn't cause Rafe any more pain than he'd already endured.

A half hour later when Shannon returned to the Rocky R, she found Rafe's car gone. For a moment she panicked. He wouldn't go back to Salinas without telling her, would he?

Common sense overcame the panic, and she reasoned that it was more likely he'd taken Janine into town or to Sacramento. Last evening after supper she'd found him hooking up his computer to the phone line. He'd explained curtly, "Sam's downloading files to me."

She knew Rafe couldn't wait to leave. The thought hurt so much it was almost a physical ache.

Spotting Clancy coming out of the barn, she headed that way. "Hi," she greeted him. "Do you think you'll get the stalls cleaned out before you leave?"

"Yep. Jim's going to be late tonight. He said he

can't pick me up until seven and wanted to know if it was okay with you if I hung out here after I finished up chores.''

''Sure. That's no problem. I noticed Rafe's car's gone. Do you know what time he'll be back?''

Clancy shrugged. ''I heard him tell Cora not to wait supper. He said he was taking Janine to the movies and didn't know where they'd end up.'' Clancy shot Shannon a curious look. ''It isn't any of my business, but he said he and Janine are leaving on Sunday.''

''Yes, they are.''

''You and he don't seem as friendly anymore.''

That was a mild way of putting it. ''We had a disagreement, and he's angry with me.''

''He should be happy you got his kid talking,'' Clancy said loyally.

''It's a lot more complicated than that.''

''Yeah, it always is with grown-ups.''

Forcing a smile, Shannon commented, ''Like you never get upset or angry.''

Clancy grinned at her and pointed to his chest. ''Not me. I just wish—'' His thought came to a halt.

''What do you wish?''

''I never stayed with one family very long. I keep expecting Jim and Marge to kick me out.''

''Jim and Marge aren't like that.''

Clancy shrugged. ''It doesn't matter. Two more years and I'll be done with school and out on my own.''

Clancy might act as if Jim and Marge's feelings didn't matter to him, but they did. He just didn't want to admit it. Too tough. Too proud. Too scared.

''Would you like to have supper with Cora and me?

I don't know what we're having yet, but there's always enough for one more.''

Clancy smiled at her. ''Sounds good.''

Shannon went to her office, told her aunt she was back and that she'd start supper. At Cora's raised brows, she didn't stick around long enough for her aunt to ask her questions. She didn't have any answers. Going to the house, she prepared a meat loaf for supper and shoved it into the oven with three baked potatoes. Seeing a bowl of peaches on the counter, she decided to make peach cobbler. Maybe cooking would keep her mind off everything else.

Clancy joined them for supper and, as Shannon sat beside him, she thought she smelled cigarette smoke. She hoped she was wrong. He didn't need to pick up a habit that could last a lifetime. After supper she'd talk to him about it.

But she never got the chance. Rafe and Janine came home just as Shannon was dishing out dessert. The tension between her and Rafe as he walked into the kitchen was tangible enough for Buster to feel it. ''How was your afternoon?'' she asked brightly.

Janine came over to the counter beside her and looked with interest at the peach cobbler. ''I liked the movie. Dad didn't. He thought it was silly.''

''The movie was fine,'' Rafe said in a gruff voice.

Janine gave him a look that daughters often give fathers when they say something totally nonsensical.

''Did you have supper?'' Shannon asked.

''We ate at Twin Pines.''

''But we didn't have dessert.'' Janine looked up at Shannon with a hopeful smile.

''How about peach cobbler with vanilla ice cream?'' Shannon offered.

Rafe raised his brows. "I thought you said you were full."

"This looks good," Janine told him.

"And I have plenty," Shannon assured her. "Come on, take a seat and I'll get the ice cream."

She knew she'd have to force down every bite. She knew she'd have to avoid Rafe's gaze. She didn't know if she could keep the truth about the baby from him.

Switching off his laptop computer, Rafe closed it and checked the clock to the side of the bed 11:00 p.m. There was no point in turning in. For the past week he hadn't gotten to sleep before 3:00 a.m. Nine days actually. Since the night—

Pushing the laptop onto the bed, he swung his legs to the floor. Shannon would be in bed by now. At least if he went downstairs onto the porch to get some air, he wouldn't feel so caged.

It was damn hard to stay away from her, but stay from her he would. He was still angry. He'd never imagined she was the type of woman to want to trap a man. Since he'd had time to think about it, he'd pretty much decided she wasn't. More likely, with her independent streak, she'd decided she wanted a baby and saw him as the easy way to get it. Stud service. That's what she'd used him for. And he didn't know how often or how long. If she'd deceived him about using the diaphragm once, she could have deceived him about it the whole time.

He ignored the whisper inside his head that told him Shannon was an honest woman.

Digging his hands into his jeans pockets, he crossed to the window and stood there. Not a whit of air was moving. Still... Did he smell smoke? Couldn't be, could it?

Going out into the hall, he checked on Janine, then quickly went down the stairs. No sound broke the night stillness, and he was relieved. If he ran into Shannon dressed in her nightshirt—

He blanked the thought from his mind, along with the sense of betrayal he felt. He still remembered the fleeting expression on her face when he'd raised his voice. How could she ever be afraid of him after the way he'd held her and touched her and kissed her?

For the umpteenth time he told himself none of it mattered. He would be taking Janine home on Sunday and they'd both forget about Shannon Collins and the Rocky R. Janine had already told him she didn't want to leave, but he'd given her a list of things to look forward to when they got home. A list of things they were going to do. They would have their lives back again.

Thanks to Shannon, that small whisper reminded him.

Rafe unlocked the front door and went out to the porch. For an instant he thought his eyes were playing tricks on him. Then he realized the orange glow on the right side of the barn was fire! Flames licked at the old structure, flaring higher and faster the longer he watched.

The horses. The fire hadn't spread to their side of the barn yet, but with those old wooden shingles on the roof—

The thought galvanized him into action. He went back inside and ran down Shannon's hall, throwing open her door. He yelled, "The barn's on fire. Call 911. I'm going out to see what I can do."

She sat up in bed. "Rafe?"

"Call 911, Shannon. Now."

Rafe thought about the horses, but he thought about his daughter, too, and how all of this could frighten her. He ran to the bunkhouse. Hearing the hum of Cora's air-conditioning, he knew she was probably fast asleep. Instead of going to the office door, he went to her bedroom window and rapped on it—hard.

In a few moments she came over to it and lifted it. "What's wrong?"

"There's a fire at the barn. Go up to the house and keep Janine inside. I'm sure Shannon will be down here as soon as she calls the fire department."

Cora turned away from the window to dress.

When Rafe raced to the barn, he heard the whinnying inside. The fire had started across the roof. He had to get the horses out for Shannon.

First he ran to Marigold's corral, unlatched the gate and sent her into the large pasture. Then he rushed to the barn.

When he opened the barn door, it was as hot as blazes inside. He headed for the stalls. He would take the horses out one by one, hoping he had enough time to get to all of them. Gray Lady was in the stall farthest from the door. Going to the first stall, he opened the gate.

When Rafe emerged from the barn with Rock-A-Bye, he brought the mare into the corral, opened the gate into the pasture where Marigold stood, then gave her a slap on her hind end. Rock-A-Bye didn't need encouragement to head away from the fire. Knowing he didn't have long to get the rest of the horses out since the whole roof was in flames now, Rafe raced back into the barn.

* * *

Cora was running up the porch steps when Shannon rushed out of the house still in her nightshirt, a pair of moccasins on her feet. She'd called 911. Now she just wanted to get to the barn—to Rafe and the horses.

"Keep Janine inside," she said to her aunt as they passed each other.

Shannon took off running and got to the barn in time to see Rafe going in—into the fire. She spotted Rock-A-Bye, Dancer with her filly and Marigold in the pasture. Cloppy and Gray Lady were still inside, and Gray Lady was at the end of the row on the inside stall.

Thinking only of her horse, Shannon dashed into the barn. The fire, not ten feet from the stalls now, was hot and crackling with bright-orange flames. She saw Rafe opening Cloppy's gate. Passing him, she hurried to Gray Lady's stall and unlatched the door. Lady bolted out and Shannon began coughing. She suddenly remembered—*the baby.*

Her baby.

She shouldn't *be* in here. She shouldn't be inhaling this smoke. Her adrenaline had been flowing so fast she hadn't thought of anything but helping Rafe, getting the horses out—

She turned to run out the way she'd come in, needing to gulp fresh air and clear her lungs. When she heard a strange cracking, she looked up.

As the beam crashed down, she backed up and covered her head with her arms. It missed her. But, fiery and heavy, it trapped her.

"Rafe!" she yelled with all the voice she had left in her. She prayed he could hear her above the roar of the fire and called for him again.

She struggled to push the beam from where it had jammed against the stall, but then she quickly let go, her hands stung by the heat from the fire burning at the other end of the beam. She felt tears rolling down her cheeks. If she got out of this, she'd tell Rafe about their baby. She'd tell him how much she loved him.

The flames crackled, burning higher, as Rafe sensed rather than saw Shannon pass the stall he'd entered to grab Cloppy's halter. Tugging the pony into the walkway, he gave her a push toward the door and then swatted her rear and ran back to help Shannon. Before he passed the next stall, he heard the horrific sound of the roof giving way and felt fear crush his chest. Gray Lady came at him wildly just before the crash. But Shannon wasn't with her.

He called Shannon's name as he made his way to the back stall.

Then he heard her calling for him, and he was never so glad to hear anything in his life. Even the fires of hell couldn't have kept him from getting to her.

She was separated from him by a fiery crossbeam.

His heart fell to his stomach, and in that instant he realized how much he cared for Shannon. How much he loved her. Loved her. Loved her.

The echo resounded in his head and around him.

He quickly surveyed the burning beam. He had to get Shannon out of here before the place collapsed on top of both of them. Scanning the area through the smoke, he spotted a pitchfork propped inside an empty stall. He rushed to it, grabbed it and tested its endurance. It might work…it had to work.

His strength came from his love as he managed to lever the handle of the pitchfork under the jammed beam. Then he pushed on it with all his might.

After a few shoves, the jammed end fell to the ground. Again using the handle of the pitchfork, he scraped the beam along the ground until he could get through to Shannon. Then, scooping Shannon into his arms, he rushed toward the barn door, grateful they were both alive, grateful he'd have the chance to say to Shannon everything bursting inside his heart.

When he rushed outside, Gray Lady whinnied a few feet ahead of him. Then she took off toward the other horses in the pasture.

He heard sirens wailing in the distance. Help was coming.

Carrying Shannon away from the smoke and the fire, he laid her down on the grass near the fence and knelt beside her. She was coughing and so was he. But she'd pulled herself to a sitting position.

"Are you hurt?" he asked, his voice raspy.

Her gaze met his, and there were tears rolling down her cheeks. "I'm fine. I was just so scared—"

Then his arms were around her, and he was rocking her. Her arms circled his neck, and she was holding on to him as desperately as he was holding on to her.

His throat was so tight he couldn't swallow, and he knew that didn't have anything to do with the smoke from the fire. Leaning away, he looked into her shining brown eyes, still brimming with tears. "I was afraid I'd lost you. I was afraid we wouldn't get out."

"Lost me?" Her tears made tracks in the soot on her cheeks. "You can't lose me, Rafe. I love you so much." Her voice broke, and she stopped. But only for an instant. "I never meant to hurt you or deceive you. What I did was so stupid, and I guess a little desperate. You were going to leave, and I thought if I couldn't have you, maybe I could have your baby.

A baby would be a part of you I could keep.'' Her voice broke in a sob.

When he'd arrived at the Rocky R, he'd been suffocating in grief and guilt and anger. Layers of it. It had started falling away, almost immediately, day by day and week by week, as he spent time with Shannon. But he hadn't wanted to acknowledge that he'd felt more than desire for her.

Seeing her torment, the sorrow and apology in her eyes, he admitted why he hadn't been able to reach out to her since that night. ''I thought you just wanted a child of your own. I thought it didn't have anything to do with me.''

''It had *everything* to do with you,'' she said with heartbreaking fervor. ''But I knew you weren't ready to love again.''

He caught one of the tears rolling down her cheek with his forefinger. ''I didn't think I was. But seeing you almost killed in a burning barn has brought me to my senses. Love isn't something that happens because it's convenient. If you wanted my child so desperately, maybe you want me, too, faults and all, in spite of my trying to lock you out of my heart.'' He saw the hope in her eyes, and he wanted to give her so much more than that. He wanted to give them both a future. ''Will you marry me, Shannon?''

''But you don't know—'' she said.

''I know all I need to know. I know you're a wonderful woman...passionate and giving.''

She shook her head and her tears fell even faster. ''I'm pregnant, Rafe. That changes everything. If you're not ready, if you don't want a baby...''

A father. He was going to be a father again. The thought shook him...almost as much as the possibility of losing Shannon. It only took him two heartbeats to ask, "Not want the baby? Shannon, I know you might think that, because of everything I've said…and done. Until now I've been fighting against my feelings for you. That fire in there—you getting caught in it—made me realize I want a future with you. *Of course* I want our baby. You're giving me a chance to start life all over again."

"But can you forgive me for what I did?" she asked with so much doubt he cursed himself for being blind for so long. "Will you trust me again? I'm so sorry—"

"Yes," he growled, "I can trust you. And I more than forgive you." There was only one way to convince her—one way to show her how much he needed her. His lips sealed to hers and then he kissed away any further apology.

When he finally broke away, Shannon's hands were in his hair. He tried to brush soot from her cheeks, but only streaked it more.

"I've got to explain something to you," she murmured.

She still looked troubled, and he didn't want anything to be a barrier between them. So he waited.

"That night we fought," she went on, her voice quivering, "and you were standing over me beside the bed…for a moment, just a moment, it was like I was thrown back in time, and my father was standing there yelling at me. But the next moment I was so relieved it was *you* who was doing the yelling. Because I *knew* you'd never hurt me. I knew I never had to be afraid of you. That night my father's ghost vanished for good. You've *got* to believe me."

Deep in his heart he'd known all along that Shannon

was an honest woman. She hadn't wanted to use him. She'd loved him so much she hadn't wanted to let go. He understood that now and he loved her for it. He wanted to help her banish all her ghosts, just as she'd helped him banish his. He hadn't been able to protect Nancy because he was only human. He wasn't a knight on a charger; he was a man. Shannon understood that and loved him because of it.

Stroking her hair, he strove to reassure her. "I believe you, sweetheart. And I love you. *Will* you marry me?"

"Are you sure?" she asked him. "So much has happened tonight. I don't want you to feel obligated because of the baby."

With determination he took her face between his palms. "I told you I loved you and asked you to marry me *before* you told me about the baby. The baby's a bonus. I'm asking you to marry me because I love you. I don't want to lose a moment with you. Time's too precious. Love's too precious. I've been thinking about opening a general law practice. What better place to do that than Fawn Grove?"

For the first time since Rafe had met her, Shannon was absolutely speechless. Finally she responded, "You'd move your life for me? For us? I can take the horses anywhere. If you want to stay in Salinas and become D.A...."

"I want you and Janine and the new baby to *be* my life. Here at the Rocky R."

Sirens wailed much closer.

"Are you going to give me an answer?" he prodded. "Or are you going to keep me waiting?"

"Oh, Rafe. Yes, I'll marry you! Yes!"

His arms still kept Shannon close as the emergency vehicles veered onto the Rocky R's access road. He glanced that way and saw Janine in her nightgown, running across the yard toward them, Cora and Buster not far behind.

His daughter rushed to them, her eyes wide as she took in the fire and the horses in the pasture and the two of them in each other's arms. "Cora said you were okay, but I wanted to see."

With one arm still around Shannon, Rafe opened his other to his daughter. "We're fine. Everything's fine. How would you like to stay here and live at the Rocky R?"

"You, too?"

"Oh, yes. Me, too. With Shannon. We'll be a family."

Janine sank to her knees between them. "You really mean it?"

Curving her arm around Janine, Shannon hugged her. "We mean it."

Cora and Buster joined the circle then, too, and as fire engines screeched to a halt, Rafe knew the process of rebuilding would be an exciting one. For all of them.

He bent his head close to Shannon's and murmured in her ear, "I love you."

As firemen ran with hoses to the barn, as paramedics came rushing toward them, as Cora looked pleased and Buster licked Janine's face, Shannon returned the words he ached to hear. "I love you, too."

Epilogue

One Year Later

Shannon was sitting on the porch, her three-and-a-half-month-old daughter on her lap facing her as Clancy bounded across the front yard toward the porch. Looking past him to the rebuilt barn and the indoor riding ring, she thought about how much her life had changed in the past year. Three weeks after the fire she'd married Rafe. His love, his caring and his commitment had changed her existence and brought her unbound happiness. She expected to see his car coming down the lane at any moment.

After Clancy ran up the porch steps, he stopped when he saw her with Amelia. Clancy had changed, too, over the past year. He'd come to her the day after the fire with his foster dad and told her the fire had been his fault. When Jim had picked him up the day of the fire, Clancy had hastily snuffed out a cigarette and tossed it to the ground. The fire marshal had figured it must have smoldered between two hay bales for hours until they burst into flames.

Shannon and Rafe had both seen how scared Clancy was, how sorry and how determined to own up to what he'd done. So Rafe had spoken to the authorities on his behalf and had stood beside him as the judge gave him a year's probation. Over the school year the teenager had worked at the Rocky R every day after classes and on weekends, at the court's direction. This summer he'd worked full-time. Clancy had given all the hours freely and with commitment, to make up for what had happened. In the process Jim and Marge Brenneman had decided to adopt Clancy officially. The sense of belonging had given the teenager a hope and confidence he hadn't had before.

Whenever he was around Amelia, he always seemed a little in awe of her. "She sure grows fast," he said now with a smile. "It seems like only yesterday you brought her home from the hospital, and she was all red and crinkled up."

Shannon laughed. "At least she had hair." Her hair was black like Rafe's, but it was fine and curly like Shannon's. "In a few months she'll be crawling. By the time you graduate she'll be walking."

"I never thought it would happen," he murmured.

"What?"

"That I'd graduate. Jim and Marge want me to take the SAT and actually think about college."

"It sounds like a plan."

"I should be working here full-time for the next ten

years to pay you back for the barn,'' Clancy mumbled, and lowered his eyes.

"Clancy, look at me. We've talked about this before. You can't pay me back for the rest of your life. Over this past year you've worked as hard as Rafe and I have to keep the Rocky R in shape, and I appreciate that. But soon it will be time for you to move on."

He looked clearly embarrassed. "Well, I'm not going anywhere for a while. Marianne sent me up here to ask you if you want to go over your schedules for next week. If you do, she'll stop up before she leaves."

While Shannon and Rafe had worked on plans for the barn and the indoor ring, she'd thought more and more about her pregnancy and where she wanted her practice to go. Marianne had always been interested in equine assisted therapy, so Shannon had asked her if she wanted to join her and become a partner. She had in the spring, a month before Amelia was born. Marianne and Cora were Amelia's godmothers, and Shannon knew she couldn't have better ones.

Shannon's office door slammed, and Shannon caught sight of Janine and Buster running toward the porch. To Clancy she said, "Tell Marianne she's invited to supper. We can go over the schedules then. Do you want to stay?"

"No. I gotta get home tonight. Jim and I are going to a go-cart race. But thanks, anyway. I'll go tell Marianne what you said." After he jogged down the steps, he gave Janine a high-five. He was becoming a big brother to her.

When Rafe's daughter came up onto the porch, her pigtails bobbed. She was tanned, her cheeks were rosy and, even more important, she was putting all the trauma in her life behind her.

"Can I hold her?" she asked Shannon.

Shannon moved to the side of the swing and patted it.

After Amelia was settled in Janine's lap, and she had both arms around the little girl's waist, she rubbed her chin in the baby's hair. "She's so soft."

"I'll bet you were just as soft when you were a baby."

Ignoring that comment, Janine informed her, "Cora says she has just a few more bills to print out and then she'll be up."

Cora was busier than ever, managing the offices of two psychologists, as well as baby-sitting, but she insisted she loved doing both.

There was the rumble of a car engine and the crunch of gravel as Rafe drove his black SUV down the lane. He'd traded in his Lexus, deciding the SUV was much more practical—just as he'd traded in his suits and ties for jeans and a Stetson. He'd opened his general law practice in Fawn Grove and said his clients didn't care how he dressed. When he appeared in court he wore a suit, of course. But this hadn't been one of those days.

After he parked, he came around the side of the house and up onto the porch, briefcase in hand. "Hi, peanut." He gave Janine a hug and kissed the top of Amelia's head. Going over to Shannon, he set the briefcase beside the swing, passed his gaze over her gauzy sundress with its flowing skirt, then gave her a slow, sweet lingering kiss that told her in no uncertain terms he wanted plenty of time alone with her later.

"Missed you," he whispered before he straightened.

"I missed you, too."

Pushing his Stetson higher on his forehead, he lounged against the porch railing. "So…what have you two been up to?"

"I helped Cora learn all about her new printer," Janine piped up.

"And I saw clients this morning and spent the afternoon with Amelia. Janine helped me feed her and give her a bath."

"Sounds like a busy day all around. I took on two more new cases for Safe Haven."

Rafe had been doing pro bono work for them, and Shannon knew he felt it was worthwhile.

"Can I ask you something? Both of you?" Janine asked.

"Ask away," Rafe encouraged her.

"School's starting soon."

"In about two weeks," Shannon prompted.

Janine looked from one of them to the other. "I was wondering…"

After a long pause Rafe asked, "What were you wondering, peanut?"

"Last year, at the end of school, we had that Muffins and Moms Day. Remember?"

Shannon remembered. When they'd gotten the notice, she'd asked if Janine wanted her to go, and Janine had told her she did. They had talked about Nancy then. After they had come home from the breakfast, Janine had gotten out a photo album that Rafe had brought to the Rocky R and looked at pictures of herself and her dad and her mom.

"I remember that day," Shannon said.

"Well, I was wondering. Clancy's getting adopted. He told me now Marge and Jim will be his mom and dad. Well…" She hesitated, then rushed ahead. "My mom's not real anymore. I mean, I have her pictures and all, but she's in heaven. So I was wondering, can Shannon adopt me and be my real mom?"

Shannon felt tears brim in her eyes. There was nothing in this world she'd like better. Her gaze went to her husband's. This decision wasn't just hers to make.

There was a world of emotion on his face as he pushed himself away from the railing and clasped Shannon's shoulder. "That sounds like a very good idea to me. But it's up to Shannon."

Shannon moved closer to Janine and put her arm around her. "You've just given me a great honor, asking me to be your mom. I would *love* to be your mother."

Grinning from ear to ear, Janine wriggled on the porch swing. "Can you take Amelia back now? I want to go tell Cora and Marianne and Clancy."

As Shannon scooped Amelia back into her arms, Janine ran down the steps, and Buster clambered after her.

Feeling a bit shell-shocked, Shannon looked up at her husband.

With a smile he sat beside her and wrapped his arm around her. "You're already her mom. This will just make it official."

"It means so much…"

Rafe drew Shannon to him, baby and all. When he kissed her again, they renewed every promise they'd ever made to each other.

After he broke away, he said hoarsely, "I never imagined I could be this happy."

"Neither did I."

He kissed her again. They were lost in each other...until someone cleared her throat.

"A fine thing for you two to be doing in front of your daughter," Cora teased.

Shannon and Rafe broke apart.

"In fact..." Cora said with a sly grin, "it's so fine, that I think I'd better watch Amelia tonight after Janine goes to bed, and give you two some time alone. What do you think?"

"I think you're one of the wisest women I know," Rafe assured her.

With her arms around her daughter, Shannon snuggled into Rafe's shoulder, knowing she was loved, knowing Rafe Pierson had brought her so many gifts she would never be able to count them all. They'd healed each other's hurts and found a love so true they would cherish it forever.

* * * * *

Be sure to look for the next book from

Karen Rose Smith

available in March 2002
from Silhouette Romance.

CALL THE ONES YOU LOVE OVER THE HOLIDAYS!

Save $25 off future book purchases when you buy any four Harlequin® or Silhouette® books in October, November and December 2001,

PLUS

receive a phone card good for 15 minutes of long-distance calls to anyone you want in North America!

WHAT AN INCREDIBLE DEAL!

Just fill out this form and attach 4 proofs of purchase (cash register receipts) from October, November and December 2001 books, and Harlequin Books will send you a coupon booklet worth a total savings of $25 off future purchases of Harlequin® and Silhouette® books, AND a 15-minute phone card to call the ones you love, anywhere in North America.

Please send this form, along with your cash register receipts
as proofs of purchase, to:
In the USA: Harlequin Books, P.O. Box 9057, Buffalo, NY 14269-9057
In Canada: Harlequin Books, P.O. Box 622, Fort Erie, Ontario L2A 5X3
Cash register receipts must be dated no later than December 31, 2001.
Limit of 1 coupon booklet and phone card per household.
Please allow 4-6 weeks for delivery.

I accept your offer! Please send me my coupon booklet and a 15-minute phone card:

Name: _____

Address: _____ City: _____

State/Prov.: _____ Zip/Postal Code: _____

Account Number (if available): _____

---

097 KJB DAGL
PHQ4012

If you enjoyed what you just read,
then we've got an offer you can't resist!

Take 2 bestselling
love stories FREE!

Plus get a FREE surprise gift!

Clip this page and mail it to Silhouette Reader Service™

IN U.S.A.
3010 Walden Ave.
P.O. Box 1867
Buffalo, N.Y. 14240-1867

IN CANADA
P.O. Box 609
Fort Erie, Ontario
L2A 5X3

YES! Please send me 2 free Silhouette Special Edition® novels and my free surprise gift. After receiving them, if I don't wish to receive anymore, I can return the shipping statement marked cancel. If I don't cancel, I will receive 6 brand-new novels every month, before they're available in stores! In the U.S.A., bill me at the bargain price of $3.80 plus 25¢ shipping and handling per book and applicable sales tax, if any*. In Canada, bill me at the bargain price of $4.21 plus 25¢ shipping and handling per book and applicable taxes**. That's the complete price and a savings of at least 10% off the cover prices—what a great deal! I understand that accepting the 2 free books and gift places me under no obligation ever to buy any books. I can always return a shipment and cancel at any time. Even if I never buy another book from Silhouette, the 2 free books and gift are mine to keep forever.

235 SEN DFNN
335 SEN DFNP

Name	(PLEASE PRINT)	
Address	Apt.#	
City	State/Prov.	Zip/Postal Code

* Terms and prices subject to change without notice. Sales tax applicable in N.Y.
** Canadian residents will be charged applicable provincial taxes and GST.
All orders subject to approval. Offer limited to one per household and not valid to current Silhouette Special Edition® subscribers.
® are registered trademarks of Harlequin Enterprises Limited.

SPED01   ©1998 Harlequin Enterprises Limited